THE LAST FIRST KISS

THE LOUDON SERIES

LUCINDA RACE

MC TWO PRESS

BOOK FOUR

The Last First Kiss
Book Four
The Loudon Series
by
Lucinda Race

Copyright © 2021 Lucinda Race

Manufactured in the United States of America Second Edition

Cover art by Meet Cute Creative

ISBN E-book 978-0-9862343-6-1

ISBN Paperback 978-0-9862343-7-8

ACKNOWLEDGEMENTS

For my daughters
True love is a rare and special gift

For Rick
For giving me a once in a lifetime look as I walked down aisle

*K*ate slammed the trunk shut, threw a duffle bag into the back seat, and slammed that door too. How could he think she was going to follow him like a lovesick puppy to Crystal Lake? Climbing behind the wheel, she pulled away from the curb, tires screeching in protest. Kate had to focus on driving and cautiously negotiated the car-lined street. Side streets in Providence were always crowded, and typically it didn't bother Kate, but today each time she had to navigate around another parked car it was like fingernails on a chalkboard.

Finally, Kate reached the highway and put her foot on the gas pedal. She fought back tears, which threatened to spill from her emerald eyes. Her long dark hair was secured in a scarf as the breeze from the open windows tugged at the stray strands. All she could think about was last night and the fight she had with the man she thought was her forever guy.

It had started over a casual dinner, talking about Kate's upcoming interview as an assistant chef in Boston. It was an amazing opportunity. Kate had dreamed of moving to a city after graduation from culinary school. She had already delayed the interview to spend some time with Donovan Price, the handsome wine salesman from Crescent Lake Winery. They had gone down state to Newport for the day and sat on a bench overlooking the ocean. It was peaceful. The sky was azure blue and the blue green waves crashed against the rocky shoreline. In the mid day sun there was a light salty breeze to keep them cool. The couple held hands cherishing the moment. They went to dinner at their favorite pub and then it happened. The fight. The couple drove back to Kate's college apartment in silence.

Don intended to help her finish packing the last of the boxes.

"Kate," Don was going to try again, "Why don't you skip the interview in Boston? I know a couple of restaurant owners and you could get a job closer to my family's home. We could see each other every weekend. I know during the week it would be tough since I'm on the road, but weekends we could explore the countryside and do whatever."

"Don, I've busted my back the last four years for an opportunity to even get an interview like this. You want me to cancel. Move to a small town I've visited a couple of times, and work where exactly, for someone who hires me as a favor to you? I don't think so." Kate threw books into an open box, "Why did you wait until tonight to bring this up? Were you afraid of what I would say?"

Don seemed surprised at Kate's anger.

"Kate, this is the next logical step. I'm sorry. I thought you'd be happy to live in the same town, instead of stringing a couple of days together every few weeks."

"I'm not angry you want to spend more time with me but your solution is for me to relocate. Why don't you move to where I live, is that too much to ask?" Kate's anger was at a rolling boil. With hands on her hips, she faced him. "Are you saying that if I don't move to Crescent Lake or somewhere in close proximity that we're through?"

"That isn't what I said. Stop putting words in my mouth. With my sales territory, getting to Boston won't be any easier than Providence. I want to spend more time with you to see where our relationship might go but we can't do that if we are a couple of hundred miles apart."

"Considering I have no intention of cancelling my interview on the off chance that one of your friends will hire me, this conversation is over. I would like you to leave. NOW!"

"Kate, you're overreacting. We can keep seeing each other."

She folded the top of the box and shoved it to one side.

"Kate! Look at me. Talk to me!" Don pleaded with her. "I don't want us to break up."

The temperature in the room plunged with each passing minute. Don made one last attempt, "Kate, please." Getting nowhere he turned on his heel and left.

Once she heard the door shut, Kate rushed over, turned the deadbolt, and dropped to the floor.

*D*on stood on the other side and could hear Kate's heart-wrenching sobs. They broke his heart. For a long time he stood there waiting and praying she would open the door. The minutes dragged until the realization hit, Kate wasn't coming after him. With a heavy heart Don plodded to his car, lost. The only place he could think to go was home to Crescent Lake Winery.

K ate lay curled up on the hard, wood floor with her cheek pressed against it. She cried until there were no tears left. She pushed up to a half sitting position and glanced around, shadows had filled the room. How long had she been there and why hadn't Don come back? Slowly she stood, and grabbed onto the table. Once she felt steadier she slowly crossed the room to the kitchen, opened the refrigerator, illuminating the small room, to find a solitary bottle of water. She opened it and took a long drink. Kate sank into a lawn-chair that sat in the middle of the room, thankful she hadn't put it in the car already. She desperately wanted to call her mother. She glanced at her watch but it was too late; her mom woke up early to open her coffee shop, What's Perkin. She walked with heavy steps into the bedroom, flopped on the bed and fell into a dreamless sleep. Her last thought before exhaustion won, she had to get the job in Boston, she didn't have anything left.

---

*K*ate woke from a deep, dreamless sleep, confused. Why was she still in her clothes and on top of the blankets, and then she remembered the argument with Don. She jumped up, frantic to find her cell phone, hoping there was a text or voicemail waiting for her.

Turning the contents of her bag onto the floor, she picked it up only to discover the battery was dead. Wildly she searched through several other bags to find the charger. She plugged it into a wall socket and then waited for her phone to turn on. Hope turned to despair when the screen indicated no missed calls and zero voicemails. Fresh tears filled her eyes, what had she done? How could she have sent the man she loved away over a job interview? Anger replaced the tears. She wiped her damp cheeks with the back of her hand and pushed a stray lock of hair off her face. She was going to that interview and she was going to get the job! Scooping the contents of her bag off the floor she left the phone charging and dashed into the bathroom. She didn't have much time to get ready and make the drive to Boston.

Kate pounded the steering wheel in frustration. She was lost. Driving up and down narrow cobblestone and brick streets. They were quaint but definitely not made for speed. Now she was driving in the wrong direction on a one-way street. Kate pulled into an alley to turn around and squeezed her small hatchback into a parking space. The only thing left to do was call and see if she could get directions from her present location. It certainly wasn't smart to keep driving in circles.

A pleasant sounding woman answered the phone, "Chops, how may I help you."

"Hello, this is Katelyn McKenna and I have an interview today but currently I'm lost and I have no idea how to get to the restaurant."

The woman said, "Just a moment and I'll get Mary to assist you."

Hold music filled Kate's ears as she tapped the steering wheel.

"Hi Kate, this is Mary Richards. Where are you?"

"I can't see a street sign or intersection." Instead, Kate described the buildings that surrounded her.

Mary's musical laughter calmed her. "I have been lost there myself. Not to worry. You are a couple of minutes away. Take your first two rights, then, take a quick left. You'll see valet parking. Pull in and give the attendant my name. He'll take your car. We're across the street, come in the main entrance and I'll be waiting for you."

Kate scribbled the instructions down as fast as Mary talked. Berating herself for missing the turns, at least Mary didn't sound irritated; she was really late. Kate put the car in gear and inched out into traffic.

"This is much worse than Providence," she muttered. After making three turns, Chops was sitting where expected. Kate pulled up to the valet and started to explain about her conversation with Mary.

"Are you Kate McKenna?" he asked.

Kate nodded and opened the driver's door. "I guess you're going to take my car and I'm going over there." Kate jabbed her thumb in the direction of the restaurant.

The valet said, "Good luck," hopped in Kate's car and didn't give her a backward glance.

Kate ran a hand over her hair to smooth any stray locks and then tugged on her suit jacket coat, fastening the button to complete the tailored look. It also gave Kate a moment to compose herself for what was to come, her first formal job interview. Kate looked right and left and crossed the street silently cursing the three-inch heels as she picked her way over the cobblestones. She hesitated, took a deep breath and pulled open the door to enter. Taking in the deep wood paneling and New England inspired artwork covering the walls, Kate felt a distinct air of tradition. Chops had been a fixture of the Boston food scene for generations. Would they offer the assistant position to a recent graduate, even if it was from one of the best schools in the country?

"Ms. McKenna?"

Studying the artwork, she hadn't heard the woman come up behind her. Kate turned and extended her hand, "Yes, Katelyn McKenna. I am very sorry I'm late." Kate babbled, "I planned extra time to get here but there was construction and a detour and that was all it took to throw off my directions."

She gave Kate a sympathetic smile. "Yes, we do have a great deal of construction. Actually, it has been going on for years." Firmly shaking the younger woman's hand, she said, "Mary Richards. Welcome to Chops. Would you follow me? I thought we'd sit in the dining room and talk."

Mary Richards had a reputation for being tough as nails. The petite, soft spoken, perfectly coiffed woman who greeted her wasn't at all what she had been expecting. Kate followed like a sheep.

Mary pulled out a chair and gestured for Kate to sit. "Coffee, water?"

"Water please." Kate took a heavy cut glass, "Thank you."

Mary waited for Kate to set down the glass before speaking, "Did you bring a copy of your resume?"

Kate pulled it from her satchel, "Yes, here it is."

Mary put on wire framed glasses and scanned the document before setting it on the table. Removing her glasses she gave Kate a stern look. "So, tell me, what makes you think you're Chops material?"

"I graduated top of my class at Johnson and Wales. I've had several successful internships; the details are on my resume. I have excellent references from the general managers and I have included letters from a couple of my professors." Kate pulled several envelopes from her bag and passed them to Mary.

Without glancing at them, Mary waited for Kate to continue.

Kate stammered, "I would like to work at Chops because it is one of the top-rated restaurants in the state and I think I could learn a great deal here."

Mary leaned forward in her chair, "So we hone your skills and what special talents do you bring to us? What sets Katelyn McKenna apart from the other fifteen applicants I've had today, other than, they were on time."

Swallowing a lump in her throat Kate knew the time was now. She had to sell herself to this woman, it didn't matter where she was in the academic lineup at graduation. "Ms. Richards, if you honor me with the opportunity to work at Chops, for starters I will never be late again. I should have driven in last night, which was my mistake. I am an excellent chef. My palate is sensitive which some may think of as a burden but I find it a fascinating challenge and I appreciate the subtleties that can elude others. I would like to request that you provide me the opportunity to show you what I can bring to your kitchen."

Mary Richards closed the folder in front of her and waited several long minutes. "Before your unfortunate detour through the city you were my top candidate. However, as much as I'm fascinated by your reputation, and it does precede you, I don't think there is a place for you at Chops. At least not at this time."

Dejected Kate fought back the tears that desperately wanted to flow. "I'm sorry you feel this way, but I understand. May I request you keep my resume on file and if there comes a time you'd like to reconsider my application please let me know. I would be interested in an opportunity."

Mary gave a curt nod, "I appreciate your tenacity. Most people shrivel up once rejected but I have a strong suspicion you appreciate my position on tardiness. I will keep your resume on file and if I rethink my decision, I promise, you'll be the second to know." Mary pushed back her chair and stood up, signaling the interview was over.

Kate once again extended her hand as she rose from the chair. "Thank you for meeting with me and your candor.

Of course, I'm disappointed but I sincerely hope to hear from you."

Kate retrieved her bag and Mary escorted her to the door.

Sitting in the car, she cried. Finally the tears stopped. Kate knew where she would go next, due west. After a detour to Providence, it was time to go home. To Loudon.

3

*C*ari McKenna's house phone was ringing as she entered the back door. She grabbed it from the hook with a quick hello as she glanced around the spacious kitchen. Her youngest daughter, Ellie, had to be home as there were breadcrumbs covering the counters. "Katie, what's that, you're on your way here? Today?"

Kate shouted into the phone, "Yes, I should be home in time for dinner. It's okay if I move home for a while? I didn't get the job in Boston."

"Of course honey, this is always you're home."

"All right then, see you soon. I should be there in about an hour." With a quick goodbye, Kate disconnected.

Cari grabbed the sponge, wiped down the counters, and rinsed the sink.

"Ellie!"

"What Mom, I'm doing my homework."

"Can you come in here for a minute. I'd like to talk with you without having to scream." Cari wondered when her baby girl became a slob.

"Hi Mom." Ellie flashed her most charming smile. "Am

I in trouble with the state of the kitchen. Especially since it had been clean when you left this morning?"

Cari ignored her question. It made no sense to belabor the obvious.

"Kate is on her way home. She'll be here in time for dinner and it sounds like she's moving back. Have you talked with her recently?"

"Nope, not since we saw her at graduation. What happened with the Boston gig, I thought that was a sure thing."

Cari shrugged, "I'm not sure. She said she didn't get the job and asked about moving home."

"Kate didn't mention Don? Weird." Ellie chewed on her lower lip, something she did when trying to figure out a problem. "I'm sure we will find out at dinner. By the way, what are we having? I'm starving."

"How can you be hungry, the counter looked like you had a feast for a snack."

"That wasn't all my crumbs. Shane stopped by on his way to look at a job or something. Oh and he said he'd be back for dinner tonight." Ellie grinned, "Just the way you like it Mom, all your little chicks at the dinner table."

Cari hated to admit it, but Ellie was right. She loved having her kids together and feeding them. It had been twelve years since the McKenna family had gone from five to four. Her husband and their dad, Ben, died of an aneurism and when Kate went off to college the house had gotten considerably quieter. That was something Cari hadn't been ready to deal with. It was unfortunate Kate's plans had changed but for Cari it meant she had a little more time to adjust to her children growing up.

Ellie danced out of the kitchen, "I've got a huge paper

to finish, call when dinner's ready or when Kate gets home."

Cari finished wiping the counters and turned to the refrigerator, unsure what to make for dinner. She poked around for ingredients in the freezer, ground beef and Italian bread. "Spaghetti and meatballs it is," she said.

The aroma of pasta sauce greeted Kate. She dragged two heavy bags over the back deck towards the kitchen door. She would get the rest tomorrow. The drive from Providence was long and exhausting. She replayed her argument with Don over and over and then blamed him for not calling and making her late for the interview. If they hadn't had the fight she wouldn't have overslept and she would have had extra time to find Chops. But no use crying over spilled milk. She was home and her mother was making her favorite dinner.

"Hello, anyone home?" Kate called.

*C*ari popped out of the back pantry with two jars of peaches in hand. "Kate!"

She set the jars on the counter, pulled her girl into a bear hug, and kissed both cheeks. With a mother's keen eye, it was easy to see her daughter had been crying and it didn't take a genius to know it wasn't over a job. "I'm glad you're home. How was the drive, Sweetheart?"

"Fine. I'm happy to be home and even happier that you're making pasta. Did you make meatballs too?" Kate picked up the lid of the heavy cast iron pot, inhaling deeply she said, "Now that's dinner."

"And, I'm going to whip up peach cobbler for dessert."

"Another favorite, you're spoiling me."

"It's in the mother's handbook. Chapter one paragraph

two, right after love each child more than you think possible. Spoil each child with favorite foods when they come home from college." Cari reached out to cup Kate's cheek, "Do you want to talk about it honey?"

Kate shook her head. "No, maybe later. Right now, I'd like to see Pixie and unpack. Is she home?"

"I think she's in the sun room, writing a paper. But I would guess she's watching television too. You know Ellie, has to have noise when she studies, not at all like you, it had to be quiet like church."

"I'll find her." Kate gave her mom a quick kiss, "Thanks Mom for being right here when I needed you."

"It's part of the mommy code. Go find your sister and I'll call you when dinner is ready. Oh, and Shane's coming over tonight."

"Good."

Kate dragged her bags into the hallway and dropped them at the bottom of the staircase. Following the sounds of an afternoon talk show Kate discovered her sister surrounded by textbooks, the television up loud. Ellie, totally oblivious to anything other than what she was concentrating on.

"Ellie." No response, "PD." Again, no response, "Pixie Dust!"

"Huh, Kate!" Ellie hopped off the couch and leaped at her sister. "When did you get here?"

"Just now." Kate turned the pad over, "What are you working on?"

"A paper for English, boring."

The girls couldn't be more different in looks but their smile was pure McKenna. Ellie was petite, blond, and deep blue eyes. Kate looked like her twin brother Shane who was tall, slender, brunette, and was blessed with emerald eyes, a striking contrast between siblings.

"Since when is English boring for you? You love high school."

"Oh I love school but it's too easy. I've talked mom into letting me take college courses next year. I'll earn credits and have more challenge. Win, win for me." Ellie plopped back on the sofa, "So what's going on with you. I thought you were going to move to Boston and wait for Don to propose."

"That was my plan, but what do they say about the best laid plans?" Kate looked out the window over the back yard. "Mom started her vegetable garden, looks like it's going to be even bigger this year."

Ellie crossed the room, wise beyond her years.

Kate's tactics of avoidance were legendary but she needed to talk.

"You know mom, it keeps her busy, between the shop and gardening she's happy."

Kate dropped her voice to a hush. "Don and I had a fight, and we broke up. I think it's over."

"Katie, people don't break up over one fight. I'm sure you'll talk and all will be fine. Has he called you yet?"

Kate shook her head, "Nope. I don't think he's going to either. We went to Newport yesterday and he said he wanted me to move to Crystal Lake, you know where his family has their winery?"

Ellie nodded waiting for more of the story.

"Well, I reminded him I had the job interview at Chops. He said one of his friends would give me a job. Like it was no big deal and that my dream to work at a five-star restaurant wasn't important. He said it would be easier for us to spend time together, he would travel during the week, and we could see each other on weekends. I got so angry I told him I wasn't moving and I didn't need his help to find a job. Besides, weekends are busy in the restaurant business. So when I would have free time he'd be doing his salesmen thing."

"It sounds like you two had a communication breakdown. But is it really the end? You know the phone works both ways."

Before Kate could answer Ellie they heard Cari call them. Shane arrived and dinner was ready.

"Pixie, don't say anything to Mom. I'll tell her when I'm ready. Okay?"

"I won't say anything tonight. But, don't wait too long Kate. Mom is a good listener and she usually has pretty good advice. But don't tell her I said that. It's never good when she thinks I'm actually paying attention. I have to keep the up the teenager and Mom game."

Kate laughed. "It will be our secret."

---

4

*S*hane enjoyed time spent with his mother and sisters but he was glad to escape to the solitude of his apartment above his mother's coffee shop, What's Perkin. About a year ago, he talked his mother into letting him renovate and convert the storage space to a two room and one bathroom apartment, it wasn't large but it was his and he relished the privacy. It was time for a little mother and son separation.

Shane parked his truck at the bottom of the stairs. He was curious what was going on with his twin sister. When Shane had talked to Don, he had gotten the impression long term plans were in the works for the couple. Shane thought Don was a stand-up guy and good enough to date his sister. Kate moving to Loudon was an unexpected twist and she wasn't saying what happened, yet. Tomorrow he would make a point of tracking her down to find out what happened and how he could help.

~

*K*ate groaned. Sunlight streamed into her childhood bedroom. Irritated, she got up and pulled the shades. Kate flopped on her stomach, foot hanging off the edge of the narrow bed and she pulled the covers over her head. It was too early to get up. For the last four years, it was work late, get up early for class. Sleeping in was a much-deserved luxury.

*C*ari arrived home. And Kate's car was parked in the same spot as this morning and the house was silent. Glancing around the kitchen she noticed nothing was out of place. She wandered through the house looking for her daughter. The sunroom was empty, and with one foot on the stair Cari paused, listening. Silence. Ascending the heavy carpeted steps she called, "Kate?"

Cari noticed the bathroom door was open and Kate's bedroom door ajar. Pausing to listen, Cari pushed open the door surprised to see a rumpled bed with Kate sprawled on top of the covers.

"Katelyn," her voice sharper than intended.

A soft hiccup answered her.

Cari sat on the edge of the bed. "Do you feel okay?"

With a sniffle, Kate mumbled into the pillow, "Yes."

Cari rubbed her back, "Honey, do you want to talk?"

No answer.

Cari had never seen Kate stay in bed all day, even as a child when she was sick she was up and around. Cari waited patiently, stroking long dark locks alternately rubbing her back, hoping Kate would open up to her.

Shadows crept into the room before Kate rolled onto

her side. Cari was shocked to see red puffy eyes looking back at her. She reached out and smoothed back Kate's bangs. "What's wrong?"

Kate pushed herself to a sitting position and grabbed a tissue; blowing her nose, she dropped it on the floor. "Don and I broke up and I miss him more than I dreamed possible, and I didn't get the job at Chops." She wailed, "My life isn't turning out anything like I thought. Mommy, what should I do?"

Cari put two and two together. "Well," She hesitated. "Do you think laying in bed all day solved any of your problems?"

Slowly, Kate shrugged her shoulders. "I guess not," she said softly.

"What is your plan for tomorrow?"

"I don't have one, why?" Kate dried her eyes. "I guess I need to look for a job."

Cari waited a few minutes, "I could use some help at What's Perkin, if you're interested. Of course it would be just until you line up a few interviews and figure out what is next."

"It would be something to keep me busy." Kate perked up. "Can I tweak the menu a bit." Kate held up her finger and thumb to demonstrate.

"We can talk about that tomorrow when you get to the shop. We start serving at seven." Cari raised an eyebrow wondering what Kate would say about starting very early.

"I remember. Can I ride in with you?"

Cari stood up, "I leave at ten of six." She turned and hid a smile as she left the room. Calling over her shoulder Cari said, "You might want to clean up this room. Dinner will be ready in thirty minutes."

Kate sat in the middle of her bed and wondered what

just happened. She had been perfectly content having a pity party. Within a few minutes she had been told to clean her room, just like when she was a teenager and given a summer job. She marveled at her mother's skill. There was still much to think about and one thing was for sure, staying in bed all day had only made her feel worse. Time for a hot shower and a home cooked meal.

*C*ari heard the shower shut off and glanced at the clock, not bad, twenty minutes. She finished tossing the salad and set the bowl in the middle of the small round table next to the bread basket. It would be several more minutes before Kate would appear. Cari poured a glass of white wine and set the bottle on the table. Taking a small sip, she sat down in the chair to wait.

"Ben, our girl has come home with a broken heart. This is a first for Kate. Everything has always turned out exactly as she planned; now, she didn't get the job or the guy. Don't worry, I'll do my best and be supportive." Cari heard slippers scuffing down the hallway and she fell silent.

"Hey, were you just talking to someone?" Kate scraped the chair over the floor and plopped down.

"Just myself. Wine?"

Kate looked at the bottle and poured some. "What's for dinner? I'm not very hungry. I hope you didn't go overboard."

"Salad, grilled shrimp, and French bread." Cari sat across from the young woman, studying the wine she swirled in her glass. "We should talk."

Kate stared out the back window, "There's really nothing to say. Don thought I should drop everything and run after him to Crystal Lake, totally dismissing my dream to work in Boston. We had a horrible fight. He left. I got lost driving into Boston and didn't get the dream job. That pretty much sums up the last few days." Kate picked up her glass and drained it, and poured a refill.

Quietly, Cari asked, "Did you ever talk about where you might move after graduation?"

"Of course. I've been talking about Chops since I was a sophomore, long before I met Donovan. I certainly didn't keep it a secret from him. I assumed he would spend more time in Boston with me, it's still part of his territory, so it made sense."

"To you but did the two of you actually talk about your future plans as a couple?"

Kate chewed her bottom lip, "Maybe? Bottom line, I thought we were on the same page and when he told me I could have a job in some restaurant in a small town that I have no interest in living, I got mad." Kate glared at her mom, "Do you think I was wrong to stand up for myself?"

"Did you stand up for yourself or draw a line in instant dry concrete? To me it sounds like you flew off the handle, maybe from the pressure of the interview. Nonetheless, you and Don didn't talk about the issue, and you told him to leave, correct?"

Kate fiddled with her fork, eyes downcast. She didn't want to admit it, but that is exactly how things had evolved. She sniffed. "Maybe."

"I take it Don hasn't called you and you haven't tried to reach him."

"Nope, no calls, e-mails or text. I guess I blew it big time." Kate wailed, "Oh Mom do you think Don *will* call me?"

"Don loves you. But you both need time to sort out

your feelings." Cari reached across the small table, and placed her hand over Kate's. "I would guess your reaction surprised him and he's upset too. Don't dwell on the fight, but reflect on what you could have done differently. Time heals all hurts, this one included."

Kate listened to her mom and a few things made sense. Feeling a little better, she gave Cari a tentative smile, "Let me grill the shrimp so we can eat. Is Ellie coming home for dinner?"

"No, she and Shane went for pizza."

Kate nodded, an old family tactic, when one kid needed some one-on-one with their mom the other two ate pizza. She was still feeling down, but the extreme heaviness in her heart was lightened just a little.

5

*B*uzz, buzz, buzz. The alarm clock emitted a piercing sound. Kate slapped it knocking it to the floor. She swung her legs over the side of the bed and waited, summoning the energy to stand and then she stumbled to the bathroom.

"Who's idea was it for five?" she muttered. Kate pulled the water on in the shower and stepped under the spray. Shrieking she flipped the lever to warm. As the water coursed over her, Kate relived the argument with Don, one more time.

"I wasn't out of line, he was! I'm not dwelling on this one more minute! It's over and I'm moving on with my life."

Kate finished getting ready and stomped down the stairs.

Summoning a half-hearted smile, she said, "Morning Mom."

With a sharp eye Mom could see past the surface and knew Kate spent a restless night.

"Morning, ready to go?"

Kate tossed Mom her keys. "You're driving."

After the short drive to the shop, Mom parked in the back at the kitchen entrance. "It's been a while since you've opened up. Do you remember what to do?" she teased.

Humorless, Kate replied, "If you haven't moved the stove or coffee pot I'm good."

When Kate entered the familiar kitchen she visibly relaxed. She got started on the morning checklist. Mom went into the front of the shop, flipped on the lights, and got the coffee brewing. She looked around the space. Pride evident on her face. Sun poured in the curtain-less windows. Above the door, the half-moon stained glass refracted a rainbow of colors over the honey hued knotty pine floors. An eclectic array of tables and chairs were randomly placed throughout the room but Kate knew each table was placed with a clear view of Main Street and a passerby could see inside and get drawn into the cozy space.

Mom walked over to straighten a photo. Her best friend, Grace Bell, was an amateur photographer and she was happy to display Grace's work. On several occasions, someone would buy a print. Grace said each photo held a tiny part of her soul.

Satisfied that the shop was ready for another day Mom poured two mugs of coffee and walked into the kitchen. She smiled happy to discover Kate had several batches of muffins and sweet breads in the oven.

"Mom, I've been thinking. I don't want to dwell on what happened. This is my new dream, to be home and working with you."

"Kate, I'll respect your wishes but I'm always ready to listen if you change your mind. Selfishly I'm happy you're here. When you're ready to talk about those ideas you mentioned, just let me know.

She grinned, "I was hoping you'd say something like that." She held up a pad. "I'm making notes. Maybe Sunday afternoon we could have a short meeting."

"It certainly didn't take you long to shake things up around here." Pleased Mom headed to the front door. "Time to open."

"I'm ready, and Mom we have a breakfast sandwich special, an egg wrap with bacon and cheese." Kate shrugged, "It's the best I could do with what you have on hand."

Kate could hear her mother laughing over the tinkling of the bell on the door. At least for today, Kate thought, she was doing okay.

She was up to her elbows in sudsy water when Shane walked into the kitchen.

"Hey Sis, I hear you're making breakfast wraps today. Any chance I can get a couple to go?"

"Yup, just give me a couple of minutes. I just finished baking some biscuits. Rumor has its strawberry picking is going strong at Blake's Farm Stand. I suggested Mom put the chalkboard out. I'm hoping people will stop in and pick some up for shortcake."

"I suspect once people know you're in the kitchen, no offense to Mom's cooking, people are going to be emptying the shelves daily. Mom's telling everyone that comes in the shop what a great chef you are. If nothing else people are going to be curious to taste for themselves." He chuckled, "Your legend has grown over the last few years."

"I am a pretty decent chef and baking is an art. I try to do it justice. And if it builds the business that's all that matters." Kate wiped her hands on the, ever- present, towel on her shoulder. "How many wraps?"

"Four? I'll give a couple to Tom. He's supervising the new guys I brought on to do lawns. I can't believe how many I have now. Did Mom tell you I bought two trucks with lifts? I've branched into tree work." Shane let out a chuckle, "No pun intended."

"You've really jumped in both feet with your land-scaping business. Do you regret not going to college?"

"Not at all. I like being my own boss and I'm turning a healthy profit and doing what I love."

"If you're happy then that's all I care about." Kate ruffled his dark hair. "Did you ever think if we had both been boys or girls we would have been identical?"

"Sis, I try to not think about being a girl, but yeah we look alike. I'm not sure where they got Ellie from though. She's the complete opposite in every way."

"Not everyway Shane, you both have Dad's blue eyes." She sighed, "I miss him."

Shane nodded, "I think about him all the time and wonder if he'd approve of how we turned out."

"I think he would. He'd want us to be happy." Kate handed a paper bag to her brother. "Four wraps and a couple of bananas. Eat them."

Shane left through the back door, "Tell Mom I'll stop over tonight. Around dinner time..." He flashed Kate a grin and was gone.

"Of course, at dinner. He'd rather eat at Mom's than a frozen pizza."

She walked over to the pass through and waited for Mom to finish waiting on her customer for telling her, "Shane's coming for dinner. We should grill burgers. I'm happy to do the cooking and Shane can be on cleanup."

"All right, let's stop by Blake's and get some berries for dessert. I'll wrap up a few biscuits before they sell out too." Another customer walked in ending the conversation.

Kate exhaled, "It's good to be home," she said softly for her ears alone.

6

The days were growing longer and business was booming at What's Perkin?. The daily breakfast and lunch specials proved to be a great addition to the standard menu and Kate was working on soup recipes for the winter season. She rarely thought about the breakup and disappointment of Boston. The routine she established in Loudon helped and Kate was contemplating her next move. Her own apartment.

She was doing the weekly inventory when male laughter drifted down from Shane's apartment, Sunday afternoon meant her brother was watching football. Looking for some conversation, she wandered up the stairs and rapped on the door as she entered.

"Hey Shane. Care if I crash the party?"

Shane, concentrating on the announcer, impatiently waved her in. "Sure. Guys this is my sister Kate, Kate the guys."

Uncomfortable under the concentrated gaze of one of the guys, Kate sat on the floor near Shane's chair.

"Hi," she said to no one in particular. She thought she

knew all her brother's friends, but the one staring at her had jet-black hair and deep gray eyes. Kate shifted on the floor and Jake, Shane's best friend, stood up.

"Kate, have a seat."

Happy to see a friendly face she said, "No thanks, I'm fine Jake." Kate wished she was downstairs.

"Ah, come on," Jake steered her to the well-worn sofa and perched on the arm next to her. He proceeded to shout at the referee on the screen.

Surreptitiously, Kate glanced around the room, only to discover the dark-haired guy was still watching her.

Shane glanced at his sister. He seemed surprised to see his new hire, Tony, staring at her. "Sis, you know Tom but have you met Tony?"

Kate shook her head. "Hi Tom."

"Hey Kate, are you a football fan?"

"I'm not, really. I just heard the commotion and wondered what the score was."

Shane interrupted, "Guys. The game. Tony Wells, my twin, Kate. Tony started working for me a couple of weeks ago."

"Nice to meet you Tony."

"Yeah, it's nice to meet you. Where have you been hiding?"

Kate blushed, "I'm not hiding. I work a lot." She glanced at her watch. "Sorry guys, I need to get back to it." She hopped up, and lightly touched her brother's shoulder. "Shane, see you later."

Without looking at anyone in particular she said goodbye. Then without a backwards glance she hastened down the stairs, but not before she heard Tony say, "Wow, Shane, your sister is quite a looker. Is she single?"

She stopped to eavesdrop, "Yeah, she had a bad break up a while back."

She hurried into the kitchen turned off the lights and locked up. She didn't want to be around when the game ended.

～

"*K*ate, can you cover the front for a few minutes. I need to get to the bank?"

"Sure, Mom."

Kate wiped her hands on a towel and went out front to straighten the coffee station. She heard the distinctive sound of the bell on the door and called out, "I'll be right with you." Kate turned and froze, "Don."

"Hello Kate." Don smiled, "You look beautiful." Ramrod straight his size dwarfed the room.

Kate stammered, "What are you doing here?"

"I needed to see you. I have missed you, and I love you." Don jammed his hands into the front pocket of his jeans.

Kate uttered one word, "Why?"

With a tender smile he said, "Why do I miss you, love you, or need you?"

"Yes. I mean no. Why are you here? Now, after all this time?" Kate felt her fragile heart shattering. "I've moved on, just as I assumed you have too."

"I've been hoping you'd call. I check my phone a thousand times a day and I'm done waiting."

"Did you come here with the idea I would pack my bags and run off with you?" Kate demanded.

"No."

She could see the flash of temper in Don's eyes and quickly reigned it back in.

"Kate, I don't want to fight again. I wanted to see your beautiful face. Is that so wrong?"

Before she could answer, the door opened and Tony Wells walked in.

"Hi Kate." He looked from her face to the big guy standing in front of her. "Is everything okay here?"

"Everything's fine. Don was just leaving."

Don bellowed, "I see what's going on here? Are you dating this guy?"

"Not that it's any of your business but Tony works for Shane and we've become friends." Kate looked at Tony hoping he would play along.

"Yeah that's right and we have a date on Saturday."

Had Tony slid that in to wrangle a date with her. There wasn't any chance she could deny it while she was trying to get Don to leave.

Kate swallowed the lump in her throat. "Well, we're just friends going to a movie. It's not a real date or anything."

Don turned, "Kate I'm staying in town and before I go we will talk things out. I'll be by tomorrow." He brushed past Tony, and stalked from the shop.

Shaken Kate leaned on the counter. "Tony thanks for playing along. I didn't expect to see Don today."

He walked behind the counter and handed Kate a glass of water. "So he's the guy?"

"What do you mean?"

"Shane said some dude broke your heart and based on how you looked when I walked in, he's the one."

"I guess so." Kate slowly sipped the water and composed herself. "But you didn't stop to get into ancient

31

history. Shane sent you in to pick up lunch. Isn't that right?"

Tony sighed. "Yeah. He said you'd have it ready."

Kate nodded and Tony followed her into the kitchen. She turned and literally bumped into him.

Flustered she said, "I'm sorry, I thought you were out front."

"Will you go to the movies with me Saturday. It can be as friends, and I'll do my best to be a gentleman. You can forget all about that blonde guy." Her flashed her a cocky grin.

"I'm afraid I wouldn't be good company."

"I'll take the chance. I'll meet you there, so it won't really be a date, just two new friends hanging out. Whatta you say?"

"Okay but it's Dutch treat and we're just friends. Agreed?" Kate stuck out her hand.

Tony grasped it. "For now." With a grin, he took the bag and jogged out the front calling, "Seven o'clock at the multiplex."

"Tony, don't make me regret this," She called after him.

"I must be crazy. What did I just agree to, go to a movie with a guy I hardly know?" Kate's thoughts whirled, "I know, I'll have Ellie go too. Safety in numbers."

$\sim$

*M*om found Kate in a tizzy when she got back from her errands. "Were you busy while I was gone?" she asked.

"Don was here."

"What? Did you know he was coming?" This was the first time Kate had spoken Don's name since the one and only conversation she had with Kate after showing up with her bags.

"No. And if I had known I would have been prepared. Tony Wells stopped in and Don accused me of dating him. Like he had any right to say anything about who I can date. Then he announced he's staying in town and we would talk before he left."

"Does this mean you're going to talk to him?"

"It doesn't sound like I have a choice, does it?" Kate's eyes filled with tears, "I was doing just fine before Don showed up today."

"Honey, if you were doing fine this wouldn't have rattled you. It's time you and Don talk this out so you can move forward."

Cari reached out and smoothed away a lone tear that slipped down Kate's cheek. "Don't wait too long Katie."

Kate wrapped her arms around her mother and cried her heart out.

7

*K*ate carefully applied her makeup. She wore a simple black turtleneck sweater with faded jeans and well-worn black cowboy boots. Small round silver hoops graced her ears. Her nerves were on edge, she wanted to look nice but not too nice. Satisfied with her reflection she said, "I'm ready."

Kate glanced at her watch; in fifteen minutes she would see Don. It was a short drive to the park but she was a bundle of nerves so she decided to walk. Without a word to her mother or Ellie, she left the house, and hurried down the sidewalk. She wanted to be the first to arrive, better to have the upper hand in this situation.

As she entered the park, Kate was surprised to see Don waiting on a stone bench. He stood up and waited for her to cross the grass.

Leaning in softly he kissed her cheek, "Thanks for meeting me. Coffee?" He handed her an insulated cup.

"Thank you." Stalling for time Kate took a sip. She was at a loss for how to begin the conversation. "Where are you staying?"

"The Village Inn. It's actually very nice. I guess I didn't know what to expect." The silence hung heavy in the air. "So things seem to be going good at your Mom's shop?"

She felt a smile come over Kate's face. "It's been good for both of us. We're trying some new menu items and so far, the customers seem to like the changes. Mom has more time to spend in her garden since I've taken over the kitchen and ordering."

"Good." Don toyed with his cup, "And you're living at your mom's?"

"For now. I'm going to start looking around. It's hard living independently, and then moving home again. I'm sure Mom enjoyed the extra one on one time she got with Ellie too."

"Kate, we need to talk about us."

"Don, keep your voice down. The entire park doesn't need to overhear our conversation. And to clarify, there is no us. There is you, and me. You made it clear you didn't respect my dreams for *my* future. You made plans without talking to me first. You knew I had the job interview in Boston and yet you wanted me to move where it was convenient for you." She kept her voice even.

"Over the past few months I've done nothing but think, Kate. You're right, I assumed you'd be happy to move to Crescent Lake since you were starting your career. It was thoughtless of me. Can you forgive me?"

Kate looked away, watching a little girl on the swings. "Yes. If that's all you need from me to move on, I forgive you." She stood, "We're done here."

Don grabbed her hand and attempted to pull her back to the bench, spilling coffee on his pants. Disregarding the mess he pleaded, "Wait, don't go."

"Don, you apologized. I've accepted. We don't have

anything left to say." Kate choked back a sob, "I have to go."

Don trailed after her, "I love you, and without you my life is empty."

She stopped and turned to face him. "In all the time we dated you never said you loved me. Do you think those three little words will change my mind now? I have spent months getting over you and it's been hard, really hard. But I've done it and now I'm moving on. I'm making new friends and doing what I love at the shop. And now you come here and tell me you love me, and what, I'm going to uproot myself and follow you? Is that what you want?"

"I don't know what I want, other than you. Will you at least think about the possibility of us seeing each other again? We can start slow and see how things go. It will have to be long distance for now, I'm still on the road."

Kate shook her head, "Don, we can't go backwards. We've done the long distance relationship for two years. I want to have a relationship with a man that is at least in the same county. I don't want to be fit into someone's travel schedule. Put yourself in my shoes." Her heart felt like a lead weight in her chest. "I need more than phone calls and a couple of days every few weeks. I deserve more and frankly we have very different ideas on relationships." Kate stood on her toes and gave him a light peck on his lips, "You were my first love, and I will always treasure the time we had together."

Don cupped her face in his massive hands, running his thumb over her quivering bottom lip. "I want to be your first, last and only love."

Wrenching away from him Kate ran from the park.

Don called after her, "Wait!"

Heedless of where she was going, she flew down Main

Street, wiping the tears from her eyes. She finally made it to Mom's and jumped into her car.

Kate drove for hours and finally pulled into the driveway at home well after dark. A few lights lit the downstairs. She was emotionally spent and longed for her bed.

The door handle turned before Kate could reach it. She entered the kitchen.

"Hey Mom."

Mom leaned against the counter. She gave Kate an understanding smile.

Bone weary, she said, "You didn't need to wait up."

"I know but I thought you'd be in the mood for chocolate chip pancakes."

Kate clung to her mother for support. "Ellie wants to join us if you'd like to share a stack."

Kate mustered a sad smile. "That sounds nice, we haven't done late night pancakes in years."

Mom pulled the prepared batter from the refrigerator and plugged in the electric skillet. "Chocolate chip pancakes are the cure all for broken hearts, a bad test grade, or anything else that might cause my kids to be sad."

The skillet sizzled as Mom dropped a little water in the middle. She poured the batter into circles. In a few minutes, mother and daughters would commiserate over gooey chocolate and sweet maple syrup.

"I'll go get Ellie." She kissed Mom's cheek before she went in search of her sister.

a week had passed since Kate met with Don. With each passing day, she was feeling more like herself again. On the counter was the real estate section of the paper and Kate was chewing on the end of a marker. She had circled several listings, potential apartments. Satisfied she had identified all viable options she picked up the phone. Kate wanted to make a few appointments before she told Mom.

Mom walked into the kitchen with two paper bags just as Kate hung up. "Kate would you grab the last couple of bags from the car? I stopped at the grocery store after the garden center." She took a sideways glance at the paper. "What's all this?"

"Let me get the bags and we can talk." Kate zipped out the door and quickly returned. Butterflies fluttered in her stomach and Kate wondered why she was nervous.

Mom emptied the contents of the bags and was putting items away, when she asked, "Are you planning on moving?"

"It's time to move into my own apartment. I appreciate living here, with you and Ellie, but I hadn't intended on moving back after college, it just turned out that way." Kate grinned, "But this time I'm not going far."

Mom smiled and tried to hide her disappointment. "I enjoy having my girls under the same roof. Would you like company? It's too bad Shane has the apartment above the shop, that might had been ideal."

"No offense Mom, I don't know if living and working in the same building would be a good idea." Kate brightened, "I'd love it if you came with me. You have a great eye for space." Kate finished unloading the bags, "You're okay with me moving?"

"Of course. You have lived in an apartment for the last three years and it must be hard to move back home. When is the first appointment and where?"

With a grin, Kate slid the paper in front of her mother. "In an hour and the other two are a half hour apart. All downtown."

"Very practical, as usual." Mom read the descriptions and pointed at one. "I know this building and the landlord. It should be pretty nice, can you afford it?"

"Yes, I've run the numbers. I'll need to find some used furniture but it will be fun checking out second hand stores. I was thinking maybe Ellie would want to make a few shopping trips with me."

"I'm sure she will. But you're not buying a second hand mattress. That will be my housewarming gift to you, no arguments." Mom glanced at her watch. "I'm going to fix a little snack for us. Apartment hunting is hunger-inducing work and dinner will be late. Give Ellie a call and let her know, will you?"

"Sure thing. I'm going to change and I'll be right down."

～

*M*om smiled. She could hear Kate humming as she dashed up the stairs. "Things are looking up."

"I'm impressed. You handled that conversation pretty good." Ben was sitting in his usual spot at the table.

"Hello dear, I didn't expect to see you, it's been a while." Cari crossed the room and sat down with her husband's ghost. "I suspect you've been keeping your eye on things around here?"

"I have. Katelyn is having a difficult time. However, I believe your support of the apartment will be good for both of you. While giving her a sense of stability and independence."

"Ben, it's the right thing to do, but she's fragile. What if she needs me and I'm not there?"

"She isn't moving to Mars, just a few blocks away, and don't forget she works for you. It will be fine."

Cari desperately wanted to reach out and hold Ben close. "Shane and Ellie are doing well. Ellie is taking college courses and Shane's business is booming."

Ben gave her his usual fuzzy smile, the way he looked before he drifted away.

"You're leaving me again... I miss you so very much."

"And I miss you, my love. I'm sorry my time is up."

Before her eyes, he was gone. "Oh Ben," she cried out, "these brief visits aren't enough for me!" Silence answered her.

. . .

*K*ate stood in the hallway listening to her mother talk to the empty chair as if her father was still alive. She hadn't realized it was still happening. After her dad died the McKenna children had gotten used to their mother talking to nothing, but Kate had hoped it had changed in the last four years. Alas, that didn't seem to have happened.

Kate called out, "Mom," and walked into the room, "I'll whip up something you sit and relax."

Grateful, Mom let Kate bustle around the kitchen slicing cheese and pepperoni, placing it on the plate with crackers, a bunch of grapes and glasses of iced tea followed.

"This is lovely, thank you."

"You're welcome. Did I hear you talking on the phone when I came in?" Kate carefully watched her mother.

"No. Just talking to myself. I'm the only person who wants to listen to me prattle on about nothing."

Mom never wanted her kids to worry so she never said she talked to their dad.

Kate wished her mother could share the truth, but for now, she would let it go. "I'm excited to apartment hunt, what are some of the things we should look at to make sure it's a good place?"

"The exterior of the building is usually a good indication of how the owner takes care of the internal systems. We'll make sure it's clean, and it needs to come with appliances."

Kate scanned the paper. "Yup they all have stove and fridge listed."

"We'll make sure they're clean too. There is nothing worse than a dirty oven. I remember when Grace and I spent a summer working at the shore. We shared a small apartment and we never used the stove, it was disgusting."

Wrinkling her nose Kate said, "Yuck, I don't want to clean someone else's mess either." The clock struck the half hour. "We should get going."

Kate hastily wiped up the remnants of their snack. "I'll drive and you can navigate."

Happy to have something to do, Mom said, "Take the first left after The Village Inn." Mom noticed Kate's face. "Something wrong?"

"No, Don was staying there, that's all." Kate turned her blinker on and slowed down. Gasping she almost hit a parked car. "Look!"

Mom looked in the direction of her arm. "What am I looking at?"

"Don's car is right there. What is he still doing in town?" A blaring horn brought her back to the present and she turned.

"You didn't know?" Mom was perplexed, "I thought you've been talking?"

"We had one conversation and I told him I wanted a real relationship, not something long distance. Since his job entails him to travel all the time it's better we end it now. I thought he agreed. Mom, do you think I should go talk to him?"

"That is totally up to you. Have you changed your mind and want to pick up where you left off?" Mom gave her a sidelong look. "It is unmistakable, you're in love with Don."

"You know what? I am not going to give him one more minute of my time or tears." Kate parked the car. "We are going to look at this apartment and see if this is going to be my new home." She glared at Mom, "Are you coming?"

"Kate, don't get irritated and take it out on me." Mom slammed the door and waited for Kate on the sidewalk.

Immediately Kate was sorry how she spoke to her mother. Kate recognized the situation was in her hands. Taking a deep breath, she alighted from the car. "Mom, I'm sorry."

Mom gave her a forgiving smile. "Let's look at this apartment, it looks nice from the curb." She looped her arm through Kate's as they walked up the front steps. "I love old Victorians." Mom pointed to the buzzer and Kate pushed it.

An older gentleman came to the door and greeted them with a warm smile, "Good afternoon, I'm Jim Ellis, you must be Kate McKenna. Come in, please."

Jim swung the door wide allowing the women to enter the front hallway.

Kate stepped in and drank in the wide mahogany stairwell. On the first floor, there was a door to the right and left. She looked up the stairs but didn't see any doors from this vantage point.

"There are four apartments, two on each floor. There is a common laundry room in the basement. I live here, A." He gestured towards the left-hand door. "The newlyweds live in B." He started up the stairs. Over his shoulder he said, "Upstairs apartment C is available, and D has a young mother, her husband is in the military."

Jim put the key in and turned the deadbolt. "The front door is always locked, for safety of course." He pushed open the door and Kate stood on the threshold, mesmerized.

Mom peeked around Kate. "I can see why your stunned. Katie it's perfect!"

9

"Mom, look at the windows, and the wood floors." Kate opened a door. "Closet." She pointed to the fireplace "Mr. Ellis, does it work?"

"It's piped for natural gas." Jim walked over and flipped a switch next to the mantel and flames sprang to life.

"That's nice, don't you think?"

Mom nodded and walked through a curved archway into the kitchen. "It's small but enough cabinets and an apartment size refrigerator and stove. Come look."

Kate joined Mom in the small but serviceable space.

"I like the ceramic counter tops, easy to keep clean." She peeked into the stove and saw that too was sparkling. "Is the bedroom through this door?"

Jim walked ahead of Kate. "To the right is the bath, and the bedroom has a large closet. Go on in and look around. I'll leave you ladies to get the feel of the place. When you're ready come knock on my door."

Kate and Mom wandered around the apartment, taking

in the views from the windows. Each room overlooked the side yard where vegetable and flower gardens were in full bloom. "What do you think Mom?"

"It's beautiful and Jim Ellis seems like a nice man. What do *you* think? It would be your apartment. You need to be comfortable."

"I really like it and it is in the middle range of my budget. I'm going to take it."

Mom laughed. "We have two more appointments,"

Kate interrupted, "What if someone else comes along and takes it. I don't want to lose this one."

"Honey, if this is the one you want then cancel the other appointments and sign the lease."

Kate did a little jig bouncing from foot to foot. "Let's go find Mr. Ellis." She slowly turned around the room. "Hopefully I can move in next weekend."

Kate floated down the stairs and knocked on Jim's door. She heard him call come in. She pushed the door open to find Jim sitting with a large fluffy cat on his lap.

"Hi Mr. Ellis, I'd like to take the apartment."

"That's just fine Kate. Please call me Jim." He pointed to the round oak coffee-table. On top lay a partially filled out form. "I thought the apartment would suit you so I took the liberty of filling in the paperwork. We're a fairly quiet bunch but the kind of neighbors you can borrow sugar from when necessary."

Kate read the page. "This is straight forward."

"All that is required, pay your rent on time and be a good neighbor so that we can live under the same roof peacefully." Jim passed her the key, "When do you want to move in?"

Kate grasped it tight. "This weekend. I'll talk to my

brother to see if he can get some of his friends to move my furniture."

"Well if I can be of any help to you, don't hesitate to ask. My phone number is on the lease and you can find me puttering in the gardens most days."

"Thank you so much and I'll drop a check by later today, if that's okay?"

Kate shook Jim's outstretched hand, "Perfect. I'll be here all afternoon."

Kate and Mom went back upstairs. Kate pulled her cell out and dialed. Making two calls in quick succession she let the other apartment managers know she had found an apartment and thanked them for their time.

"I wish we brought a tape measure, we could jot down the size of the windows and get some blinds tomorrow."

Mom rummaged around in her handbag and held up a tape, victorious! "Why wait?"

"Is there anything you don't have in that bag? You're just like Mary Poppins!" Kate took the tape and the pad and pen she dug out.

"I've told you before about the mom code. Now let's get the measurements and get home so I can see what furniture will work in your new place."

"Mom, I'm planning on second hand stores and yard sales. I don't need you to give me stuff from your house. Well except a bed." Grinning, Kate finished up and reluctantly locked the door. "I can't wait to show Ellie my place."

Mom called Shane from the car. "Hi, have you had dinner yet?"

"Hey, I was just going to fix something why, are you offering?"

"We'll have dinner in about a half hour, if you can stop by Kate needs to talk to you about using the truck and man power. She rented a place on Baker Street, in that gorgeous Victorian."

"Sure, I'll swing by and I have something I need to talk to her about anyway. I'll see you soon."

"Your brother's coming over and everything is coming together."

Kate's smile could have lit up the town. "Yes, it is. As soon as I get settled, I'm going to have the family over for dinner. Well, when I have enough chairs."

Kate pulled into the driveway, "Thanks for your help today, and I'm really sorry I was a little testy. Seeing Don's car bothered me more than I thought."

Mom seemed to choose her words carefully. "Honey, you need to focus on your future and not the past. Believe me I know better than anyone how hard that can be, but you have to figure this out, not for Don but for you."

"I'm working on it. The apartment is the next big step."

Ellie was in the kitchen, making a salad. "I got Kate's message and Shane called and said he was picking up ice cream. Since we're having a family dinner, I decided salad would taste good. Did you get an apartment in the Victorian?"

"Yup, the one on Baker Street and I'm moving this weekend, so you'll be back to being the only kid at home and have Mom to yourself again."

"Jeez, I finally just got used to you being back and now you're moving. Can I have a key?"

"Seriously? You want a key?"

"Well I have a key to Shane's place and of course here. I just figured in case you needed me to do something you wouldn't have to worry about getting me a key then." Ellie didn't see what the big deal was. "It's not like I'm looking for a place to have a party or something."

"Have you ever been to a party?" Kate teased.

"Of course I have but I don't have time for juvenile events. All the kids do is drink and stuff." Ellie sniffed, "That just isn't my thing."

"Pixie, chill. I was teasing you."

"I don't think you're very funny." Before the conversation could continue, Shane breezed into the kitchen.

He held up two bags. "Hello ladies, I come bearing ice cream and sundae fixings, including, drum roll please, chocolate and rainbow sprinkles."

"Fudge sauce and whipped cream too?" Ellie dug into the bags. With a squeal she pulled a jar of caramel sauce out. "Can we skip dinner?"

Mom's gaze slid from face to face to face. "This reminds me of when you were younger. You know house rules, nutrition before sweetness."

"Mom, you do know Kate used to eat ice cream for breakfast, she added a banana and call it breakfast split."

"Really? I had no idea. Any other secrets you care to share?" Mom gave each child her famous look.

Sheepishly, Ellie shook her head, "I've been sworn to secrecy." And then giggled, "And you can see how that worked out."

"No worries El, Mom can't ground Shane or me. So be careful you don't spill any more secrets that could get you in trouble."

The four McKenna's rolled up their sleeves and put dinner on the table. There much teasing and joking between the twins and Ellie. As usual, Shane had a soft spot for his baby sister and would steer the conversation to a new topic when she started to get upset.

"What is your school schedule like this semester Ellie, still top of your class?"

"I guess so, I talked with my guidance counselor today about graduating early. I have all my required courses down and I'm taking two freshman college classes so to me it's logical I graduate from high school and get on with my life."

"But you'll miss out on prom and all the other stuff that goes with senior year," Shane said.

Kate sighed, "I loved my senior year."

Kate, you and Shane loved high school. You played sports and were in clubs, but to me I'm wasting time. Besides I don't even know if they'll let me." Ellie looked at her mother for support.

"Ellie and I have talked, if the school agrees then I'll agree."

Kate didn't understand why her mother would agree but decided to save this conversation for another day.

"Shane, Mom said you had something you wanted to talk about?"

He pushed away from the table and set up the ice cream bar. "You need help this weekend moving?"

"I'm going to start moving small stuff in the car, but yeah, I need to move a bed and if I can find a sofa I'll need some muscle."

"Sure, I can ask Jake to give me a hand too." Shane scooped ice cream, dumped caramel and fudge sauce on the top and then gave a liberal shot of canned whipped cream.

"Ah Kate, I hired a new guy today."

"Really, I didn't know you were looking for help. You just hired Tony Wells, didn't you?"

"I did but he moved on. So that left me a man down."

Unsure where this conversation was going she said, "Well I'm glad you found someone."

"Kate, I hired Don."

*a*fter the momentary shock, Kate glared at Shane.

"How dare you!" She rushed from the room, with Ellie close on her heels.

Shane sank onto a stool and looked at the floor, "That didn't go as bad as I thought."

"What did you expect, that Kate would throw her arms around you and thank you for hiring her ex-boyfriend?" Mom began clearing what was left of dinner. "What were you thinking."

"You think I'm interfering, and I guess I am. But I've talked to Don, several times over the last few months and hurt wasn't a one-way street. He loves Kate. This was a huge misunderstanding and you know Kate, once she gets something in her head, even if she's wrong, she won't change her mind."

Shane wiped down the table and tossed the sponge into the sink and leaned against the counter. "How many times did she break up with a guy for something minor? And what about the time she stopped seeing that guy because he teased her about becoming his personal chef, that wasn't exactly reasonable thinking. Mom, you have to agree when things aren't going exactly as Kate plans, she bolts. Don said they didn't talk about the future and what would happen after graduation and Don agreed he was a jerk and assumed she would follow him. But he knows what he said was wrong. He loves Kate so much he walked away from his family's business to move to Loudon. He intends on winning her back and I'm going to help him."

"If this doesn't work out the way you have planned Kate will resent you for a long time."

"You have to trust me. Besides, we are all a little relationship shy. You haven't dated anyone since Dad died, Ellie buries herself in school-work and a few select friends, Kate and I keep people at arms length. We are so worried about getting hurt we're terrified to take a chance."

Mom was silent while Shane talked about the four of them like they were pathetic.

"For your information, I choose not to date, it's not that I can't date. I have a very full life."

"Mom, I didn't mean anything by what I said. But you have to admit, we're afraid of falling in love. Losing Dad was the hardest thing that ever will happen to us. To love is to risk that kind of pain again."

Mom studied Shane. Her emerald eyes saddened by the truth of his words. "So what is your plan to get these two together?"

"Simple. Don works for McKenna Landscaping and by definition is an extended part of our family. He'll be stopping by the shop to pick up lunch from time to time, and basically, he will be around."

He placed a box on the counter and scooped up a bowl of ice cream and covered it with toppings. With chocolate sauce dripping from his spoon he said, "I'm hoping Kate will start to soften towards him and start talking. I'm not doing anything more than providing Don with the opportunity to see her regularly. It's up to him where things go. Don is going to have to woo her all over again, only this will be different from Providence, her armor will be even thicker this time around."

"And you think she'll change her mind?"

"Donovan Price is the best man for my sister. He loves her and even more, he understands what makes her tick. I can tell you there aren't many guys out there that are good enough for her. I promise you, I've spent lot of time thinking over his idea. It took several heart to heart conversations for Don to convince me to let him work here."

Ellie walked into the room. All five feet two inches was spoiling for a fight. "Shane!"

Shocked, he turned to take the full wrath from her. "Ellie, before you jump into your over-protective mode we need to talk. Have a seat."

"I don't want to sit down, what I want to do is knock the brain back into your head. Do you have any idea that Kate feels you have betrayed her and frankly, I agree!"

Shane pulled out a stool, "Have a seat." He steered Ellie to the counter and pushed her to sit. "First of all I have been thinking about this situation since June and if you haven't noticed Kate isn't *getting over* Don. Yes, she is working and moving into an apartment but take a hard look at her when she thinks no one is watching, she's hemorrhaging inside. I won't stand by and do nothing."

It was easy to see the wind was taken out of her sails. Ellie asked, "But hiring Don? Are you sure that is the right thing to do?"

"They love each other and as sappy as it sounds coming from a guy, they belong together. I just told Mom, I'm giving them an opportunity to work things out. Nothing more."

"Shane, if that is all you're doing then go talk to Kate. She's upstairs crying and she feels you took sides in something that was between her and Don."

"I figured that is how she would react." Shane picked up the shoe box from the counter. "I have something for her. Don has been writing letters and he asked me to give them to her. She can read them or not but at least he'll get the chance to nudge open her heart and mind."

"When did you bring that in?" Mom asked.

"When I brought the bags in. I dropped it behind the door so Kate wouldn't see it. I'm going upstairs and both of you should stay here. I need some time with Kate."

He strode from the room.

~

*E*llie came over and sat next to her mom. "Do you think Shane is doing the right thing?"

"Honey, I don't know what the right or wrong thing is for Kate. But I do agree with Shane she made a hasty decision in June. There was a lot happening in the span of a few days and when Kate feels overwhelmed, she's like a turtle and pulls the hard shell over her head. If she and Don don't get back together at least, this time, it won't be for lack of communication. As much as she talks, sometimes she misses the subtle point of real communication."

Unsure how to respond Ellie sat with Mom, straining to hear what was going on upstairs.

~

*S*hane rapped on the door. "Kate, can I come in?"

Through the door he heard a muffled sob. "Go away! I don't want to talk to you!"

The knob turned freely in his hand. He eased it open and saw Kate was laying face down on the bed, clutching her old teddy bear.

"Kate, I'm coming in."

Lacking for something to say she lifted her head and glowered at her brother. She saw a box tucked under his arm. "Bringing me a pair of shoes won't help."

Shane laid the box on the foot of the bed. "They're not shoes, but it is for you and there are a few things I want to say. You can listen or not, your choice."

Kate sniffed and rose to a half sitting position. "I'm here so go ahead."

When you came back to Loudon in June devastated, I wanted to throttle Don for breaking your heart, so I called him."

"You did?" Kate wiped her cheeks with Teddy.

"Of course, anyone who hurts my sister has to answer to me, just like when we were in elementary school, remember?"

Kate nodded and cracked a tiny grin. "Like the kid who cut off the bottom of my ponytail?"

"Yup, and I got in big trouble for taking his bike. Dad was not happy with me. Just like then I still am doing what I can to protect you." He held up a hand as Kate started to interrupt him. "I called Don a couple of days after you arrived. He told me what happened and that it was a misunderstanding. Setting things up for you in his hometown without even talking to you was stupid. He was hoping you'd call him so that you could sit down and talk things over. But he is very aware that you are stubborn and pigheaded. A trait we have in common, but anyway I digress, he called every week and asked how you were. I never gave him details but he knows you haven't gotten over him, just as he has not gotten over you."

"How do you know that?"

Shane pulled the box over and placed it within arms reach. "He asked me to give you this box."

Kate carefully ran her hand across the top. "What's in it?"

"You'll have to look inside." Shane stood up to leave, "Katie, I didn't do anything to hurt you. Everything I have done is because I love you and I want to see your real smile again, not that fake version you wear every day."

Kate focused on the box. Shane left the room, as she was tentatively lifting the lid.

a stack of envelopes, in various sizes and thickness, rested inside the box. Kate leafed through them; they bore stamps without post marks.

"Why didn't you mail these?" Kate turned one over and saw a small number in the bottom right. Curious she turned over a few more and saw they were all numbered. Quickly she put them in order. "Maybe I should start with one." She held it in her hand staring at it for several minutes. Sucking in a ragged breath, carefully she slit it open.

A slip of paper fell out, with a simple statement -

Kate, I love you.

Kate dropped the paper as if it burned her fingers and held back a cry. In rapid succession, she continued to open envelopes, the messages were similar, until she picked up number twelve. It was thick and contained a handwritten letter. Kate got off the bed, walked to the window seat and curled up in the corner. She unfolded the pages of the letter.

My dearest Kate,

It has been fifty-nine days since the last time I saw your beautiful face. I can't stop thinking about what I should have said or done differently. I can't go back and change the past, the only thing I can do is prepare to change our future. I check my phone and e-mail a thousand times a day hoping to discover a message from you. I am enduring the silence to give you time, but each day that passes is killing me just a little more.

When I'm driving I catch myself looking for you everywhere, despite the fact I know you are living in Loudon. I dream that you'll surprise me in one of the towns. I have even gone by your apartment in Providence, just in case you went back there. But alas, despite seeing you in my dreams that is the only glimpse I have gotten of your beautiful smile.

By now, you know I have been talking to Shane. To his credit at first, he didn't want anything to do with me and if the situation was different and it was one of my sisters, I would have had the same reaction. But I think he understands the depth of my feelings for you. I plan on asking him for a job. After seeing you a few weeks ago I know I must make a choice or lose you forever. That isn't an option for me. Life without you is no life at all.

I don't expect you to jump in my arms the first time you see me around town. However, I have every intention of showing you that I'm still the man you fell in love with, but hopefully a little wiser. I pray you'll give our relationship careful consideration and that you can find it in your heart to spend some time with me, talking for now and let's see where we can go from here.

Kate, I love you with every fiber of my being and I pray it's not too late.

Until I see you again,
Forever yours,
Don

~

*K*ate stared out the window, unsure what to think or how to feel. A light knock at the door roused her from a stupor.

"Come in."

Ellie stood in the doorway, "Would you like company?" Not waiting for a response, she perched on the chair nearest the window. "How are you doing?"

"Numb I think." Kate passed the letter to her sister. "Read this."

Ellie glanced at the handwriting, "Are you sure? I'm guessing this is a love letter and might be best for your eyes only."

"No, go ahead. I want you to read it."

Shadows had lengthened across the room and Kate flipped on a couple of small lamps, wandered to the bed and scooped up the last of the envelopes, tucking them into the cardboard box. For tonight, she had read enough.

Ellie let out a low whistle. "This is quite a letter. It sounds like he is sincere." Ellie chose her next words carefully. "What do you think?"

"I was finally adjusting to life without Don Price and here he goes and writes me this letter that basically says he loves me and will do anything to make things right between us."

"And that makes you mad?"

"Damn right it does."

"Why?"

"He is arrogant and self serving."

Ellie held up the pages. "That isn't what I read in this letter. It sounds like he regrets what happened and he loves you, and wants you in his life. Don is moving to town to be closer to you. I think that is the ultimate romantic gesture."

"Hmm, that is one way to look at it, I think it is the ultimate manipulation."

"Kate, don't be a stubborn jerk. Do you love him?"

Kate wrung her hands and plopped on the bed. "I have. From the minute he brought me cookies and iced tea in Fountain Plaza, it was all over. I knew I would love him for the rest of my life."

"So what's the problem? And you can't keep clinging to the fight, that's in the past, everyone fights sometimes."

"Maybe I'm scared, okay? The minute I graduated from college I was moving out of my apartment, going on my first real job interview and he says I should pack up and follow him somewhere. We hadn't discussed anything about our future. I didn't know if we even had one."

"It's obvious to me what he wants. Don just threw his career down the drain to work for our brother. What does that tell you?"

Kate shrugged her shoulders. "I don't know, he loves me I guess?"

"Hallelujah, the light bulb started to glow above your head."

"You don't need to be a smart aleck, El, and besides, when did you get to be such a wise old lady?"

Ellie let out a snort. "I've always been wise, and I decided long ago it was easier watching my brother and sister make mistakes and I learned from you. And for the record I make enough of my own."

"Glad Shane and I can blaze a trail for you, Pixie."

Ellie gave a mock bow. "Thank you so much Sis. But you're trying to divert our conversation. What are you going to do about Don?"

Kate stared at the ceiling. "If you were me, what would you do?"

"Are you sure you want my opinion?"

"I suppose I do. Tell me."

"I would give him a chance to court you again. Date, until you know what you want and I would strongly encourage you to be honest about what you want for your future. Where do you see your life in one, five and ten years? You'll need to ask Don too and see if you're on the same page. If you are, then let nature take its course, if you're not then cut the ties, for both your sakes, and move on."

Kate listened.

With a hushed voice she said, "I miss Don very much and in these last three months I'd hoped he would call or come see me. When he did, I became a shrew. I didn't want to give him a chance to really talk about things." Tears sprang to her eyes, "Why am I like this Ellie?"

"Fear, of being hurt by love. Now that you recognize it, face it head on and either get over it or let it consume you." She stood up. "I've said enough. I'm going to my room. If you want to talk, I'm here for you." At the door she paused, "Sissy, think long and hard about what you want and need. Follow your heart. Mom always says, your heart knows the way." Ellie slipped out of the room.

Kate pulled back the covers on her bed and climbed in, not bothering to change into pajamas and fell into a deep sleep, the first in many weeks she wasn't troubled with bad dreams. Her last thought was of her love for one man, Donovan Price.

12

*D*on peeked through the window of What's Perkin?. Debating what he should say when he walked in he spent several agonizing minutes as he stood on the sidewalk. Taking a firm grasp of the door handle he pushed it open. Cari greeted him with a genuine smile before glancing to the kitchen.

After taking a deep breath he said, "Good morning Cari."

"Hello stranger, it's good to see you." Cari walked around the counter and gave him a warm hug. "It's been a while."

"I know, I've been in town a few times and I'm sorry I didn't get the chance to see you. I'm sure you've heard the news. Shane hired me so I'll be around more." Don glanced at the kitchen, wondering if there was truth in his words or if Kate would refuse to give him the time of day.

With a reassuring smile Cari said, "That's good news." She pointed to the kitchen. "For all of us."

Don relaxed, at least one McKenna woman was happy to see him.

"I'd like to order an egg and sausage breakfast sandwich to go and of course some coffee."

Cari passed him an insulated travel mug with the shop's logo, "Use this one. Bring it with you for refills. I'll get your order."

Don glanced around the room, unsure where the coffee pot was located. He enjoyed the vibe of the shop, its mouthwatering aromas, were warm and inviting, like stepping into his mother's kitchen. He poured a mugful, added a splash of cream and a liberal dose of sugar.

A familiar voice spoke, "Price, don't you think that's too much sugar, you'll drown out the taste of the coffee."

A smile filled his face and he turned, head tilted to one side, at last, he was able to feast his eyes on Kate. "It's what keeps me sweet."

"Ah, is that what does it, good to know."

Kate wore a deep purple tee shirt, hair pulled through the back of a baseball cap with her ponytail hung down gracing her long straight back.

"It's good to see you."

The first crack in her protective shell and he'd take it. "It's good to see you too. You look great, a little slimmer, but it suits you."

"Thank you. Is today you're first day on the job?"

"No. I don't start until Monday. I'm apartment hunting, any tips?"

"Uh, no. There are several out there that sound nice. In fact I signed a lease a few days ago."

Don held his surprise in check; he thought Kate would live at home longer. "Oh, where?"

Seeing a look of distress cloud her emerald eyes, quickly he said, "I'll make sure I don't rent something in your building or even on the same street."

Relieved she answered, "Baker Street, there is a pretty Victorian and I rented an apartment on the second floor. It's really nice and I'm moving in on Sunday."

"That's good news Kate. I'm sure it's perfect." Mentally, Don crossed Baker Street off his list. "Well I'm going to head out." Don crossed to the counter and paid Cari. "But maybe I'll see you at some point."

"Sounds nice, Don. I hope you get lucky today and find an apartment."

Don grinned. "You know me, I'm determined."

Kate's face paled at the double meaning, "Well good luck." She fled to the safety of the kitchen.

Don gave Cari a tentative smile. "I'll see you around."

*M*om waited until Don was on the other side of the closed door then gave it a few more minutes knowing Kate would be out to talk.

"Mom," she hissed thought the pass through. "Is he gone?"

"The coast is clear, you can come out." Amused, Cari smiled, "So, I guess you've made a decision."

"I have." Kate stated, "I'm going to take things slow and when I see Don we'll talk and if and when he asks me out on a date I'm going to go. But we're not picking up where we left off. This is a new, budding romance and I want to make sure we can communicate and are on the same page with our dreams and goals."

"That is music to my ears. I'm glad you've taken some time to think about everything and it has given you perspective."

"Honestly Mom, it wasn't my idea to give Don a second chance. After I talked to Ellie last night, she set me straight. I knew I had to find out for sure if a relationship was Don was possible and try, if not I can let it go and move on with my life. Ellie is right, if I don't try I'll always wonder."

"I knew your sister has been paying attention, she's wise beyond her years."

"You aren't kidding. Who knew our little pixie dust was so in tune to matters of the heart."

Mother and daughter were interrupted by an influx of customers.

~

*A*t the close of the day Kate went searching for Mom. "Hey, do you want to go to the mall with me? I want to get shades and curtains for my new place. I thought it might be fun and I left Ellie a message. If she doesn't have too much homework maybe we can make it a girls night, including dinner, my treat."

"I like how that sounds. Do we have time for a quick shower before we go?"

Kate nodded. "That will give me time to review my list and see what else I want to buy." The shop phone rang and Kate picked it up. "What's Perkin."

She listened to the person on the other end.

"Okay, we'll meet you at home in," Kate glanced at her watch, "Thirty minutes?" Kate hung up without saying goodbye.

"Guess you could hear, that was Ellie and she's coming with us. Do you think a half hour is enough time?"

"Its not a big deal if we don't leave soon. The mall will still be there. This is going to be fun, your first real apartment."

Kate smirked. "So, you don't count the place at school?"

Mom shook her head, "No, that was a temporary sorority house. You didn't spend any time making it a home; it served a singular purpose, a roof over your head during college. This will be very different."

Kate murmured. "You know Mom, for the first time in a long time I believe things are going to be fine, whatever happens with Don."

"I'm glad honey. I have to admit I was worried about you."

"No need to worry, I have a great job I love, a new apartment that is the bomb and a great family." Kate grinned. "What else do I need?"

"What indeed." Mom gave Kate a one-arm hug, "Let's go shopping. There is a fabulous new kitchen store and I'm buying you a nice house warming gift while we're there."

"I like how that sounds Mom, but I don't want you spending one nickel on me. You've done enough letting me move home, giving me a job and you did buy me a new mattress."

"It wasn't a hardship honey, you're my girl. As far as the job goes, you've earned the right to run my kitchen. I love to cook but I've discovered dealing with customers is so much more fun. I get to talk to everyone that comes into the shop."

Kate grew quiet. "Mom, do you think Shane did the right thing? Talking to Don without telling me?"

"Shane did what he thought was best for you. You're his twin and you share something that I can't understand. From the time you two were toddlers he was always looking out for you, guiding you and if necessary being your protector." Mom's eyes got a faraway look. "I remember one time, I'm not sure how old you were, but you had drawn on the walls in your bedroom, instead of taking a nap. When I went up to get you, well let's just put it this way I wasn't happy. We were having a rather stern discussion and Shane came bopping in and told me that you couldn't possibly have done it because the puppy was asleep on the crayons."

"He said that?" Kate giggled, "Like Pebbles used them or something?"

Mom's eyes filled with tears from laughing. "Oh yes, and he was serious. Well I didn't have the heart to scold either one of you at that point. So, the three of us went and had a talk with Pebbles about not drawing on the walls. You leaned down, put your ear next to her mouth and then looked up at me with those big green eyes of yours. You were very serious when you said Mommy, Pebbles promises she will never do that again."

Kate chuckled. "Pebbles was a great dog, and she never did draw on the walls again."

"No and neither did you or Shane. I hope that story shows you how much your brother has always loved you and will always do what he feels is the best thing for you. Even if you don't happen to agree at the moment."

"I'm pretty lucky, Mom. I have a great family."

13

*K*ate surveyed the boxes that were in various stages of being packed. There was little hope she would be ready by eleven. She wondered when she accumulated so much stuff.

"Kate," Mom yelled up the stairwell, "Shane's here."

"I'll be down in a minute." Kate picked up a small duffel bag, grabbed a box, and jogged down the stairs. Grinning she thrust the box at her brother. "I've under estimated how much stuff has to be moved. And you're early."

"I figured you would. Jake drove his truck too so maybe we can still do this in one trip."

Ellie yelled down, "Kate does it matter what box I grab first?"

"Nope, they all have to come."

Jake poked his head in the front door and scanned the hallway, "Hey Kate, are more boxes upstairs?"

Kate nodded. Jake took the stairs two at a time almost plowing into Ellie. He grabbed the box from her and put out a steadying hand.

"You okay, Squirt?"

Ellie nodded. "Yeah, but just for that you can take all the heavy boxes to the truck. Kate isn't really packed so be careful when you pick them up. I don't know if the bottoms were taped or just folded in."

Jake leapt down the stairs with a box of books under each arm, passing Mom and Kate.

"Hi Jake."

"Hey Cari, be right back."

He called out to his dad, Ray. Mom peeked outside and gave a wave.

"Hey neighbor. Coffee?"

Ray strolled across their adjoining yards. "Good morning. I see it's moving day."

"It is. I think I'm going to let the kids handle the loading of boxes and the small furniture Kate's taking. Care to sit on the sidelines and watch?"

"Lead the way. This should be entertaining." He chuckled, "I see four bosses and no worker bees."

Kate watched as Ray followed Mom into the kitchen. They had a well-established routine. Mom would hand him a mug. He helped himself to cream from the refrigerator. Over the twelve years, Shane and Jake had spent their time in one house or the other so Ray and Mom had developed a solid friendship. Ray would wait for Mom to extend her cup where he'd add a splash of cream to her mug. The kids often wondered why they hadn't dated. Ray and Mom made a good couple.

Kate had just put a box in the back of Jake's truck when the bickering started.

"That didn't take long," Ray observed from his seat on the porch.

Ellie was handing a paper bag to Shane. "Tuck that in front of those boxes, and it will be fine."

"And I think it's better if it goes in the cab."

"Whatever." Ellie stomped off, "Kate, I'm going to check your room, and then we should go." Ellie looked at the sky. "Rain is coming."

Kate looked up to a pale blue sky peppered with dark clouds. "Guys, we should hurry. Ellie might be right, it looks like rain."

Jake and Shane moved at the same pace, they were used to Kate and Ellie pushing them.

"Go tell Mom we're almost ready and see if she's riding with me." Shane loaded the last small table into the back of the truck.

Kate walked over to where Mom was enjoying coffee and conversation with Ray. It was good to see her relaxed and better still to hear her laugh.

"We're ready, are you coming now? Shane said you could ride with him."

Mom asked Ray, "If you're not busy you could ride over to see Kate's place. It's pretty nice."

He stood up and took both mugs. "I've got nothing planned so I'll tag along. I can drive so Shane doesn't have to come back and there's plenty of room for Ellie."

"Ellie can ride with me and then she can go home with you guys. We'll see you over there?"

"Give me a minute I need to grab my handbag. Ray, I'll walk over to your place. No need to drive over here."

"Kate, you and Ellie go ahead. Your mom and I will be right behind you."

Kate crossed the lawn with a bounce in her step, "Pixie, I'm leaving."

Ellie came flying out the front door, slamming it behind her. She jumped into the car and buckled up. "Ready."

Beaming, Kate carefully backed out of the driveway.

"Are you nervous to live alone?"

"I haven't really thought about it. Last night when I was putting dishes in the cabinets, it was peaceful. I'm excited and happy. It will be weird sleeping there, but in a good way." Kate pulled a key from the cup holder. "This is for you."

"You're giving me a key to your apartment? Are you sure?"

"Of course, the lock is to keep out people I don't know and the key is to let in people I love." Kate flashed her a smile. "Ellie you're my sister and wherever I live there is always a place for you too."

"Thanks Kate, you don't have to worry. I won't just drop by and let myself in without calling first." Ellie teased, "I wouldn't want to walk in on you, well if you had a guy over or something."

"Jeez I hadn't thought of that, maybe you should return the key after all." Kate extended her hand and grinned.

"Nope, you gave it to me so it's mine now." With dramatic flair, Ellie tucked it in the front pocket of her jeans.

With a smirk, Kate pulled into the parking area and left enough room for the trucks. "Muscles ready?"

"Yeah, yeah let's go unload. I hope you have snacks I'm getting hungry."

"I got sandwiches, chips and cookies. You'll be well fed, but after we work."

Ellie called out to the guys. "She's cracking the whip, no cookies until everything is upstairs."

"That's incentive. What kind of cookies Kate?"

"You'll have to wait and see." Kate grabbed the first box, "Last one upstairs doesn't get one."

Jake and Shane hurried past her, racing each other. "Some things never change." Kate pointed to their backsides, "It's like they're still kids, trying to get something over the other."

"It's getting the job done Kate, so it's all good." Ellie waved at a truck pulling in the parking area. "Mom and Ray are here."

A rumble of thunder could be heard in the distance, "Did you hear that? We'd better hurry," Ellie said.

The family made short work of the trucks and Mom set lunch on the coffee table. Everyone flopped in chairs or on the floor.

"Water?" Cari asked as she passed out ice-cold bottles.

"Mom you forgot the cookies." Shane piled meat and cheese on a hard roll, "Pickles?"

Kate spoke up from the kitchen, "You're lucky you got meat and cheese Shane, no pickles." She entered the room with a platter of brownies, cookies and cupcakes.

"Now this is what I live for, variety." Jake grabbed one of each before making a sandwich.

With a laugh Kate said, "You know they aren't going to disappear Jake."

"Let me introduce you to your brother, he's a vacuum cleaner when it comes to sweets. If I snooze I usually lose."

"I have plenty more in the kitchen."

The group munched on sandwiches and relaxed. Kate spoke between bites; "I want to thank you for helping today and when I get settled you're all invited to Sunday dinner."

"That sounds good to me Kate," Jake piped up.

Everyone had a suggestion for the meal, which had Kate smiling. This is what she thought her life would be like. "You'll get what I cook and love it."

Mom said, "This bantering will go on for a long time between you four." She caught Ray's eye. "Whenever you're ready we can go, my flower gardens could use some attention."

"I'm ready. Ellie do you want to come with us, or when Jake is coming home I'm sure he can drop you off."

"I'll stay and help Kate unpack."

Mom leaned over to peck Ellie's cheek, "I'll see you at home."

"Shane, Jake, thank you for helping today. It didn't take as long as I anticipated." Mom finished giving each of her children, including Jake a hug, "Katie, see you in the morning but if you need something later don't hesitate to call."

"Kate suppressed a grin. "Don't worry Mom, I'll be fine, and I will see you bright and early."

～

*C*ari and Ray walked down the wide staircase. "I'm sure you must think I'm over protective, but for me it never gets easier. There are times when I'd like to wrap them in cotton and keep them locked in the house."

Ray touched her shoulder, "I know how you feel. I feel the same way about my son. After Jake's mother left I wanted to protect him from anything and everything, which, by the way, isn't possible. If you need a shoulder to lean on give me a call. Being a parent is tough, no matter how old they are."

"You speak the truth, old friend." Cari and Ray drove

home in companionable silence. "If you're interested I have some tomatoes left in the garden. You're welcome to them."

"Tempting. Are you sure you don't want them?"

"I've made all the sauce I'll need for the winter and I won't eat them fast enough before they spoil, so help yourself."

"I will, thanks." Ray stopped in Cari's driveway. "I'll walk over later."

Cari opened the truck door.

"Cari," Ray said, "Kate has a great apartment and I did a little poking around. There are sturdy locks on all the doors and windows."

"Thanks for checking those out. She's an adult and I have to remember that. Thank goodness I still have Ellie under my roof, I'm not ready for an empty nest."

"Your kids are lucky to have a great mother."

"Jake's pretty lucky too."

"I know exactly what you mean. I am dreading the day Jake announces he's moving out. The day will come but hopefully not for a while yet."

Ray put the truck in reverse and waited a moment as Cari gave a jaunty wave. Then she stooped to pull a weed in her flower garden. Maybe she'd have a glass of wine when Ray stopped over. That would be nice.

*K*ate leaned back on the sofa. She was finally alone in her apartment. Ellie had been a whirlwind of activity, getting all the boxes unpacked and flattened, and everything was put in its proper place. It had been a long day and she was trying to decide if it was cold cereal for dinner or take out, until a knock at the door forced her to get up.

She peered through the peephole. What was he doing at her door?

Thinking fast, she sputtered, "Just a minute." In an attempt to smooth the flyaway strands, she ran a hand over her hair and swung the door open. "Hi Don, this is a surprise."

"Hi Kate, I hope I'm not interrupting the unpacking but I thought you might be tired and hungry." He held out a flat white box and a brown paper bag, "I brought pizza and beer. I thought we might have dinner, as friends."

Kate hesitated, "I'm not really dressed for company." Feeling rude keeping him on the threshold, she murmured and stepped to one side. "Please, come in."

Don looked around the living room. It was bright, spacious and it reflected Kate's understated style. It looked liked a home. "This is nice, the windows go almost to the floor. Does the fireplace work?"

"It does." Kate pointed towards the archway, "The kitchen is through there and the bedroom and bath is in the back. These old Victorians have generous rooms and amazing natural light."

Don set the pizza box on the coffee table and walked to the window. "Whose garden?"

"The landlord, Jim Ellis. Apparently, he likes to putter in the yard. Aren't the flowers stunning? I haven't seen flower gardens like this in person except for Mom's."

Don nodded, "It's a nice place Kate and it suits you."

"Any luck yet finding a place?"

"I found an efficiency at the opposite end of town. For now that is all I need."

Uncomfortable silence settled over the couple.

"That pizza smells good. I'll get some plates and glasses." Kate disappeared into the safety of her tiny kitchen.

Taking a deep breath to steady her hammering heart, she placed plates, mugs, and napkins on a tray. Her mind was racing, trying to think of something to talk about that was safe topic until Don appeared in the doorway.

"Can I help?" Without waiting for an answer he picked up the tray. "Shall we?"

Kate had no choice but to follow Don. "What kind of pizza did you get?" She picked up a beer and poured. "Sorry they're not frosted." She passed a mug to Don.

"White pizza with vegetables on half and meat lovers on the other half, with extra cheese."

She smiled and her insides softened. "You remembered."

"Of course I remember your favorite pizza and beer." Don passed her a plate, "Are you going to sit down? I promise, I won't bite."

Kate sat cross-legged on the floor. "I'm comfortable."

"This is nice. Being together." Before she could answer him, Don asked, "Do you have anything left to move?"

Shaking her head and holding up a finger, she chewed a bite of pizza. "No I didn't have much at Mom's. I want to hit some second hand shops for odds and ends to finish decorating. I suspect that is what I'll be doing for the next few weekends. I want to find some curtains for the bedroom, I got shades, but they're ugly."

He snorted, "I know what that means, you'll search high and low until you find exactly what you're looking for."

Silence once again crept in. "Are you looking forward to starting your new job tomorrow? It's certainly going to be a change from what you've been doing."

"I've always loved working outside. It's good to be physically tired and I sleep better. Shane will show me what he expects when I supervise the crew. I need to get my drivers license changed so I can drive the company vehicles."

"I'm sure working for Shane will have its moments, but he's fair. At least that's what I've been told."

"I respect Shane. He took a small lawn business and worked hard to grow his company. Business comes easy to me so if he wants any advice I'm happy to oblige. I've spent my life watching my dad and he's built CLW into a major player in the industry."

Kate took another slice and put one on Don's plate. "CLW?"

"Thank you." He shrugged, "Crescent Lake Winery."

"Oh, right. I got used to thinking of it as, the winery."

"This seems like old times, doesn't it Katie?" Grinning, he continued, "Eating pizza, drinking cold beer and good conversation."

"This is nice." She put down her glass, "Can we talk about what happened in Providence? I've been giving it a lot of thought the last few weeks and I've wondered if I overreacted, if you were overzealous or maybe we're both responsible for the breakup."

He choked on his pizza.

She waited until he seemed to be breathing normally before continuing. "Sorry, I didn't mean to catch you off guard but if we are thinking about seeing each other again we have to talk about what happened. Don't you agree?"

"Totally. I'm surprised you brought this up now. You want to get into all of this tonight? This conversation is going to take more than a few minutes." Don challenged.

"Don, I need to know, are you in love with me?"

Unflinching, he looked directly into the depths of her green eyes. "I have been in love with you since the moment I ruined your chef coat. I'll never forget your eyes shooting daggers at me. You stormed off without so much as a backward glance. You were the first girl I'd met that didn't give me a second look. You were serious and determined and I found that very sexy and intriguing. And as a side note those cheekbones of yours, wow. I just had to find you and ask you on a date."

Don got up and leaned against the mantel. "But it wasn't just you're looks. You're smart, passionate about life and loyal to those you love. I couldn't wait for you to graduate. I dreamed of being able to see you whenever I wanted and in my enthusiasm, I didn't talk to you about our future. I thought you could get a good job anywhere and I didn't understand why Chops was so important to you. For that I'm truly sorry."

Kate listened. "I'm curious, why did you move to Loudon. Working for Shane is the total opposite from what you were doing."

"It is, but I love the outdoors, working with my hands, and the most important reason? This is where you live. I want to be able to see you and talk to you, even if it is just as friends. I plan on proving to you that I am not the same clod who planned our life without talking to you."

Kate's heart swelled with happiness. Cautiously, she said, "I need some time and we should date. I want us both to be sure about what we want for our future."

"I'd like that and I promise you won't regret giving me another chance." Don reached out to take her hand.

She desperately wanted to be in his arms, but that would come in time. Until then, a simple touch was enough. Kate felt the goosebumps race down her back when their hands met. She raised her eyes to gaze into the smoldering depths of Don's soft brown eyes. She longed to discover what had transpired in the last several months.

Kate chose her words carefully. "You seem different than the last time we were together in Newport."

"Really. How?"

"More relaxed, less focused on your cell phone and your schedule and you're present in this moment with me."

"Kate, I had a lot of time to think about you, me, our relationship and what I really want. If I want you in my life, I have to make significant changes and be the Don you see in front of you. To be a part of the fast paced business world I have to be the other Don, the one that is always ready to take the next call. Driving through New England there is a lot of windshield time and I had hours to ponder what I really wanted. I even thought about dating."

Kate opened her mouth but before she could say a word Don held up his hand.

"But I didn't want to ask out any other girl. Being in love with you has changed things for me. I've discovered I want things, a marriage, home and someday a couple of rug rats running around calling me daddy. Every scenario I ran through my head, you were the only girl I wanted by my side. If you told me to leave and not come back, it would take a long time to purge you from my soul, if I ever could. So here I am hoping to find my way back into your life and heart."

Tears sprung to Kate's eyes. "For a man of few words that was the most wonderful, sweetest thing you've ever said to me. I'd be crazy to send you to Crescent Lake after that speech."

Kate scrambled up from the floor and crossed to the window. She turned to Don and stretched out her hand. "Come here. Look out the window. This is my home. Do you believe you can be happy, truly happy, with this view, these people, and the jobs we will have?"

Tenderly Don pulled her into his arms. "The landscape is irrelevant. The only thing that truly matters is we are looking at the same view, together."

The couple stood side by side until stars started dotting the inky sky.

Don didn't want to break the spell but this was a new beginning, "Kate I'm going to leave now. But I promise we will see each other very soon." He kissed the top of her head, his finger slid down her cheek and tenderly he pulled her face up to his. "Sleep well sweetheart." Without a backward glance, Don left Kate's apartment.

The room felt hallow without his presence. Mechanically, Kate picked up the remnants of dinner and washed up the glasses and plates. She flipped on the stereo, filling the room with soft jazz music. Usually the melodic horns were a salve for her unsettled mood but tonight the magic didn't work. Kate clicked it off, and walked down the short hallway to her new bedroom. Tomorrow was a new day and she couldn't wait to see Don.

15

"*I*t's been three days and Don hasn't called or stopped by, do you think he changed his mind and went home?" Kate demanded to know what her mother thought of the situation.

"Don't you think you need to give Don some time, he's getting settled, started a new job and if you remember you both agreed to take things slow, right?"

Kate slammed the oven door a little harder than intended. "Yes, we did agree to go slow but this isn't slow he's nonexistent. He could have called."

"Kate, give the man some space. Now that you've decided you want Don back in your life you're impatient. Think about what you're doing and focus on the cupcakes, they are starting to smell a little over done."

She pulled the door open and smoke rolled into the kitchen. She grabbed the oven mitt and pulled out the tray and dropped it on the counter.

"Great. Ruined." Kate dumped the blackened cupcakes into the garbage and tossed the pan into the dish sink. "You're right Mom, but I don't have to like it."

The door-bell jingled indicating someone had entered the shop. Kate peered out through the window and discovered a large bouquet of flowers were on the display case. Kate let out a low whistle, "Mom, who is sending you flowers?"

"I have no idea, let me check the card. Maybe they were delivered by mistake." Mom pulled the small white envelope out of the center of the flowers, "Kate, they're not for me."

Curious, Kate came out front. "Who are they for?"

Mom handed her the card, "Take a look."

Kate giggled like a school girl. "They're for me!" Kate danced around the room with the unopened envelope.

"Don't you think you should see who sent them?" Mom teased.

Kate ripped off one edge and shook out the tiny card, "To my darling Kate. Dinner tonight. See you at seven." She turned it over, "It's not signed, but it has to be from Don."

She suddenly looked serious, "Oh my stars, what am I going to wear?"

Mom laughed, "Call your sister. She's good at picking out the perfect outfit."

Kate dashed into the kitchen and found her cell phone. Breathless she left a message for Ellie, "Hey, come to the shop ASAP, I have a hot date tonight and nothing to wear. I need your help little sis. Call me back."

She disconnected and perched on the stool and fanned herself with a towel. "Wow. I'm lightheaded."

Mom placed a steadying hand on Kate. "Take some slow deep breaths and I'll get you a glass of water."

She closed her eyes and waited for the odd feeling to

pass. A cool glass was pressed into her hand and she took a small sip. "The room has stopped spinning."

Mom hovered over her. "Just sit and take it easy. No need to rush around." Mom felt Kate's forehead and took notice of the color in her cheeks, "You're flushed. When was the last time you ate something?"

"I ate breakfast, relax. I think I was hyperventilating, nothing more serious than a bad case of butterflies."

"First time you've been so worked up over a bouquet of daisies." Mom caught sight of Ellie walking in front of the shop window. "Your sister's here."

Kate's eyes popped open and shined with excitement, "El, we're back here."

Ellie came through the door, "I got your message and came right over. Who's your hot date with? Last I new the only available man hadn't spoken to you in days."

Kate handed Ellie the card. "Take a look."

Ellie scanned the short note and her head spun around and caught site of the huge bouquet on the counter. "Whew that cost some coin. Don?"

"Of course," Kate grinned, "Ellie, I don't have any idea what to wear. Will you help me?"

"You've spent the last few years wearing uniforms and I'm sure you don't have anything in your closet he hasn't seen so I think we need to shop. Mom, do you mind if Kate leaves a little early? We could meet you at Anna's Closet when you close. I'll pick out a few outfits, Kate can try them on, and wa la, she'll have something that will make Don's jaw drop."

"I like how you think. I could scoot out in about a half hour or so, okay Mom?"

"Sure and I'll be right behind you. I want to see your sister dress you."

Ellie looked at her watch. "I'll shoot you a text when I'm ready and if I decide to go somewhere else I'll let you know." Ellie dashed out the door.

"This should be interesting. Ellie's taste isn't exactly the same as mine." Kate mused. "Maybe I should have set some parameters, or at least a budget."

"Don't worry about a budget or what she'll pick. Go with the flow and have some faith in Ellie, she has impeccable taste. This is shaping up to be an exciting night and dressing up will give you an extra boost of confidence."

"I wish the butterflies in my stomach knew the plan. All I want to do at the moment is throw up." Kate moved towards the stove, "I need to get this kitchen cleaned up and ready for tomorrow," the bell interrupted Kate's ramblings, "And it sounds like you have a customer."

Mom exited the kitchen to greet her customer. It was business as usual.

~

*C*ari hurried down the street to catch up with her daughters. She was anxious to see what Ellie had picked out for Kate. Upon entering Anna's Closet she smiled at the clerk and walked to the back of the store, towards the fitting rooms.

"Hi girls."

Ellie appeared from behind a rack, "Hey Mom. We're down to three outfits, two dresses and one pants outfit. Kate's having a hard time choosing so you can help. I have my favorite but of course she doesn't want to listen."

Kate peeked from behind a curtain. "I'm just not sure which one is the best. I'll put on the first dress." Kate disappeared and rustling sounds could be heard.

Ellie passed a necklace under the curtain. "Put this on with the purple dress."

Kate made some weird sound> "This one? Are you sure?"

"Yup." Ellie was holding a few more accessories, which Cari presumed, would go with the other outfits.

Kate pushed aside the curtain and stepped out. "Well what do you think?"

She was dressed in a charcoal gray knit dress that was ruched to one side, and a graceful scooped neckline. A three strand black beaded necklace graced her throat. The dress brushed just at the top of her knees and she wore knee high black leather boots. "It's good that Don is tall, so I can actually wear these." Kate showed off the spiked heels. "What do you think, Mom?"

"It's lovely and flatters your figure. How do you feel in it?"

"I like it but I'm not sold, it doesn't have much color." Kate studied her reflection. "I'm going to try on the pants." She tucked behind the curtain and passed the dress and necklace out to Ellie who laid them on an overstuffed chair.

Next Kate emerged with long black slacks that hugged her every move and a deep cowl neck burgundy sweater. "Well?"

Cari wrinkled her nose, "It's a beautiful outfit but not for tonight. Let me see the other dress."

"Ellie, thoughts?"

"Mom's right, definitely not for tonight."

Ellie took the cast-offs and hung them on the rack. Cari was anxious to see the last dress.

When Kate appeared she was stunned by her reflection. "This is the dress for tonight," she gushed.

Kate turned from side to side. The skirt with layers of green and purple chiffon reminiscent of a woodland fairy rustled softly. The scooped neck top was a rich plum with three-quarter length sleeves that matched perfectly to the plum color in the skirt. On her feet she wore suede pumps with bows to complete the look.

Ellie presented her with a teardrop amethyst necklace, "This is perfect, and if you put your hair up in a loose bun, all romantic looking, you'll be like Cinderella going to the ball."

Cari watched as her oldest daughter blossomed into a woman before her eyes. Whatever promise the night held, it would be an evening neither Kate nor Don would ever forget.

"Do you think Don will like it?"

Ellie squeezed Kate's arm. "Sis, if this outfit doesn't make his eyes pop out of his head, nothing will."

"Good, just the look I want to achieve."

16

*A*t five minutes to seven Kate entered the living room. Mom set her magazine aside.

"Oh Katie." Tears hovered in the corners of her eyes. "You're radiant and that dress is perfect."

A knock on the front door made Kate turn. "He's here", she whispered. She took one last look in the mirror and wiped a tiny smudge of lipstick from the edge of her mouth.

"You shouldn't keep Don waiting." Mom nudged Kate towards the door.

Kate put her hand on the doorknob and pulled it open, "Don." She drank in every detail of the man she loved. He wore a dark sport coat, a blue and white striped shirt and dark trousers.

The look in Don's eyes spoke volumes and he stumbled over his words, "Kate, you are beautiful."

A shy smile played over her lips, "Thank you. You're looking pretty sharp yourself."

"If you're ready we have reservations at The White House." Don took Kate's wrap and draped it over her shoulders. Kate picked up her clutch, kissed Mom's cheek, and stepped into the crisp fall night air.

~

*D*on and Kate were ushered to a quiet table. It was mid week so few tables were occupied.

In a hushed voice Kate said, "This is very romantic. I've eaten here once, when Shane and I graduated high school. Mom and my grandparents brought us here to celebrate. The food and the service both were impeccable."

"I wanted tonight to be special and when I asked Cari this was her first and only choice."

"Mom knows about tonight?"

"Nothing specific, just that I was looking for a five star establishment and she made the recommendation."

"Oh, I see. That explains a lot of things."

Curious about her comment he said, "Explains what?"

"I tried on a few nice outfits and she vetoed both."

"Well I'm very glad she did, you look stunning. In fact I've never seen you look more beautiful."

Kate blushed a deep shade of pink. "Enough talk about my clothes. Let's look at the menu."

"No need. I've preordered everything from appetizers, main course, dessert and even the wine."

Kate cocked one eyebrow. "Well, this is interesting. I hope you picked out all my favorite dishes," she teased.

"You didn't complain about the pizza Sunday night so I'm pretty sure you'll be pleased." Don nodded to the waiter who came with a bottle of wine. After presenting it to Don, he poured a glass for Kate and Don, placed it on the table and slipped away.

He picked up his glass and waited for Kate, "To a memorable evening."

The couple clinked glasses and she took a sip of the smooth cabernet. "Delicious, so far you're doing great."

Salad, soup, and the entrée came at a leisurely pace and conversation flowed easily. For the casual observer it was easy to see the love between the couple and for Don and Kate the love that had been simmering ignited into a roaring blaze.

Over coffee, Don took Kate's hand and caressed her palm. "I don't want to bring up a sad subject but I would like to go back to that night in Providence, after our day in Newport."

A dark cloud flitted over Kate's face and Don continued to caress her hand. "Sweetheart, indulge me. If I could turn back the clock and change what happened that night I wouldn't."

She attempted to pull her hand away. "I don't want to ruin dinner, so let's just forget about everything."

"Wait, hear me out. Please!" He held her hand so Kate had to sit down unless she wanted to create a scene. "The reason I wouldn't change anything that has happened over the last few months is, for me, it has helped me realize I will only love one woman in my lifetime. I know we talked about starting slow and dating but after the other night I need to ask you a question."

Don reached into his coat pocket and pulled out a small red velvet box. Setting it on the table he continued. "If we hadn't had our disagreement I would have given this to you in June. But I never would have discovered the meaning of soul mates and I might have taken you and our love for granted."

Don slipped from his chair and down on one knee.

Kate bit her bottom lip, holding back the tears that were building.

"Kate, almost two years ago I gave you a kiss goodnight. I want that to be my last, first kiss. I love you with all my heart. Marry me and make me the luckiest man on earth."

Don opened the velvet case and removed an antique ruby and diamond ring. "This was my Great Grandmother Price's ring. When I was sixteen Gram gave it to me, and told me one day I would fall in love with a very special woman. When I proposed I should present her with this ring and ask her to be my bride."

Tears flowed unchecked down Kate's cheeks. Putting out her left hand Don slipped it on her trembling finger. "Yes. Yes. Yes, Don, I'll marry you."

Don swept Kate into his arms. His lips hovered a mere breath from hers. "This will be the first kiss of the rest of our lives."

She closed her eyes and he lowered his mouth to hers, and murmured, "You are my life."

"And you're mine." Kate melted in his arms.

$\mathcal{T}$he happy couple had taken their time choosing a date and now wedding plans were in full swing. The big day was less than a week away. Kate had always dreamed of a church wedding, complete with family and friends in attendance. They made both short and long term plans. After the honeymoon, Don would move into her apartment and someday they would buy a home. Kate's phone rang and she glanced at caller id, happy to see her sister's name.

"Hi Ellie, where are you?"

"The more important question is where are you? You are supposed to be at the last dress fitting and to pick up our dresses. Did you forget?"

"No, I have plenty of time it's only," Kate looked at her watch. "Oh no, it stopped. I'm on my way."

Kate dashed out of the apartment and flew to the dress shop. When she entered, she was greeted with a chorus of female voices shouting, "Surprise!"

"A bridal shower, here in the dress shop?" Kate looked

around at her mother, sister, her mom's best friend Grace, and Grandma Susan. "When did you do all of this?"

Ellie handed Kate a tissue, "It was the only place we thought would be a surprise."

Don's mother Sherry and his three sisters, Anna, Tessa and Liza hugged her tight.

"When did you get to town?" Kate gushed.

"This morning and we're here until after the wedding. We can help with any last minute details or whatever you might need. We're family now." Sherry beamed.

"This is wonderful and it is so beautiful, but I still need to have a dress fitting." Kate glanced towards her mother, "But not to be rude I don't want everyone to see my dress until the wedding."

Mom smiled. "Not to worry Kate, after we have some refreshments and you open gifts we'll close the store and do our dress fittings. Relax honey, you should know by now that everything is taken care of and you can enjoy being the bride."

Glancing around the room Kate was grateful everyone she cared for was here to celebrate. She grinned, "Well then let's get this party started!"

The afternoon flew by and Kate was relaxed and enjoyed each minute, trying to savor the details so later, she could share them with Don.

Ellie perched on the side of her sister's chair. "How are you holding up? Should I start to break up the party for gown time?"

"Yes, I can't wait to see how it looks, and your dress too."

Ellie slipped off the chair and discreetly told Grace and Sherry, it was time to break up the party. Within a short time, three McKenna women and Gram, along with Sherry and her future sisters-in-law stood around the now quiet room. Michelle, the owner, joined the ladies.

"Did you enjoy your shower Kate?"

"I did very much. Thank you for letting Ellie and Mom hold the shower here. I know it had to have been a bit of an imposition."

"Not at all and I was happy to do it. Now shall we try on dresses?"

The air was filled with electricity. Michelle retrieved Ellie's dress. She pointed to a dressing room and Ellie disappeared inside.

"How's it fit El?" Mom called to her.

"Hold on, just zipping it up." Ellie opened the door and came out. "Well what do you think? Do I look like a maid of honor?"

Kate indicated Ellie should twirl. "I want to see how it moves on you."

She did as was asked showing off the shades of blue in the chiffon skirt. "I like how it moves, it is comfortable too. Mom, what do you think?"

"You don't look like the baby of the family in this dress." Mom seemed to take note of the sweetheart neckline, closely fit bodice and the skirt graced Ellie's slender legs. "You're going to look very pretty, honey."

"Thanks," and then she blurted out, "Kate, I am dying to see your dress, but let's see Sherry, Grandma and Mom try on their dresses first."

Sherry smiled as Michelle handed her a forest green dress. She quickly returned and turned in front of Kate. "Does this look okay?"

Kate gave her a hard hug. "Gorgeous."

Grandma joined Sherry and Ellie in wedding finery.

"Grandma, your dress is a wow-zer, when you said

you wanted to wear beige I never thought you'd look like this! You all look amazing!"

Finally, it was Mom's turn. She walked into a vacant dressing room with a deep purple jacket and skirt ensemble. A few minutes later she stepped into the main room.

Kate beamed. "That is perfect on you Mom, just as I imagined. It has the right amount of bling with a few sparkles in the jacket and the chiffon skirt is just perfect." She clapped her hands together.

Michelle came out of the back with a large white garment bag carefully cradled in her arms. "Kate, if you'll come with me, it's time your family gets their first look of the bride."

Kate looked at Mom, did a little dance and said, "Be right out."

Kate disappeared into the large dressing room that was designated for the bride.

*a*mid rustling, Kate could be heard softly laughing. This was music to Cari's ears. She clasped her mother's hand.

"Mom, can you believe your first-born granddaughter is getting married?"

Tears sprang to Cari's eyes and Mom patted her arm.

"I know exactly how you are feeling. It seems like it was just last week you married Ben."

"I wish he was here to walk Kate down the aisle. Don't get me wrong I'm happy Daddy is going to give her away, but well, you know."

"You don't need to worry, Dad would understand and Cari, Ben is here. He has been watching over all of you since he was taken too soon.

Conversation was cut short when the door opened and Michelle walked out first, "Here is a radiant bride."

Kate made her entrance, holding the hem of her skirt up so that she wouldn't trip. She went to stand on the elevated floor in front of the triple mirrors. Taking a deep breath she smoothed the front of the dress down, "Well everyone, what do you think?"

Cari was happy to be sitting. Her knees were shaking even in the chair. "Kate you are a vision of loveliness."

Kate had chosen a strapless dress of silk and chiffon with a sweetheart neckline. The bodice was decorated with appliqued flowers and iridescent beading. She wore a cathedral length veil with a crystal-encrusted comb in her up-do.

"How do my shoes look with the dress?" Kate held up the hem and her strappy high-heeled sandals were silver with crystals on the straps.

"They look great but will they be comfortable all day?" Ellie wondered out loud.

"I've got that covered. If my feet get tired I have sparkly flip flops. I want to dance all night!"

Ellie laughed, "It's your night so you could dance bare-foot if you wanted."

Mom and Cari stood on either side of Kate and Ellie. Sherry and Don's sisters wiped tears from their eyes.

Sherry said, "Don's a lucky guy."

Three generations of McKenna women were ready for a wedding.

"All I need to do is pray for perfect weather."

Cari put her arm around Kate. "Rain or shine, it will be a perfect day."

18

*K*ate had slept in her childhood bedroom the last night she was a single woman. When she woke, for a split second she wondered why she wasn't in her apartment, and then she remembered, it was her wedding day. The day had been busy with hair and makeup for the women. Shane would be keeping Don company along with his brothers, Jack and Leo, and his only job was to make sure the men were at the church on time. The wedding was a black tie affair and scheduled to start at five with the reception to follow at The White House. The guest list was small, family and a few close friends.

Kate sat in front of her makeup mirror. A knock on the door brought Kate out of her daze. "Come in" she called. Looking in the mirror Kate saw it was her mother. "Hi Mom."

"Hi Honey, you've been up here a while so I thought I'd come check on you."

"The insanity is running wild downstairs. I needed a

few minutes of peace in my old room. After today it's not mine anymore."

"It will always be your room, but you'll have a home with Don. I suspect when you have a daughter and she spends the night with her grandma, she'll sleep here, in her mommy's room."

"Mom," Kate whispered. "Were you nervous when you married Daddy?"

A dreamy look came over Mom's face. "I was very nervous. I distinctly remember when Grandpa came up to get me. I was standing in front of the mirror and when I turned and saw him, at that moment the nerves vanished. I couldn't wait to marry your dad."

"I wish Daddy was here to walk me down the aisle."

Mom sat down next to Kate. "Look in the mirror and tell me what you see?"

"My mother and me on my wedding day, with great looking hair," a nervous laugh escaped her lips.

Mom leaned in, "I'll tell you what I see, your father's cheek bones, the wave of his hair, the sound of his laugh in yours. In so many ways, you remind me of your dad. Close your eyes and you'll feel his love."

Kate did as she was asked and fought back the lump growing in her throat. She wasn't sure if it was her imagination or real but she felt surrounded by love and the air held a faint whiff of his aftershave.

"Mom, Daddy's here, isn't he?"

"Yes sweetheart, he has always been with you."

Mother and daughter sat side by side, savoring the moment.

She blinked away a happy tear. "I'm ready."

"Take a few minutes and I'll tell everyone its time to go

and when you're ready come downstairs. Ellie and I will be waiting."

~

$\mathcal{K}$ate stood at the back of the church, arm and arm with her grandfather. Ellie had fluffed her gown and Don's brother Jack escorted her mother and grandmother down the long aisle.

Strains of Pachelbel's Canon filled the church, the entrance doors opened and Ellie took one last look at Kate, and began her walk down the deep red plush carpet. She was half way when everyone stood in the pews. Ellie kept her eyes locked on Don's and she knew the exact moment he saw his bride. The joy on his face was reassuring that true love existed and Ellie was thrilled her sister found it.

Grandpa placed his free hand on top of Kate's, leaned in to kiss his granddaughter's cheek. "You look beautiful. So much like your mother on her wedding day."

"Thank you Grandpa. I'm ready if you are."

Kate paused at the entrance of the church. Her eyes locked with Don's and her knees grew weak. He was incredibly handsome in his black tuxedo and red bowtie. Gliding down the aisle Kate didn't hear the music or see the people, it was all a blur. Grandpa placed Kate's hand in Don's.

The minister began the ceremony. Don leaned in and whispered, "I have never seen a more beautiful bride."

Kate squeezed his hand in response.

The minister had stopped talking and looked at Kate and Don.

"Kate. Don. Turn and face each other and repeat after me."

He waited while they turned to each other.

"Don, do you take Kate as your best friend and wife for all time?"

In a deep rich baritone voice, he proclaimed, "I do."

"Do you Kate, take Don as your best friend and husband for all time?"

Just above a whisper Kate said, "For all time."

The minster said a few additional words, blessed the couple, and then declared, "It is my pleasure to introduce for the first time Katelyn and Donovan Price."

A thunderous applause echoed throughout the church. Kate and Don floated down the aisle.

"Mrs. Price. I love the red heels."

Kate grinned. "Nobody knew I was going to switch my shoes. I'm sure you don't remember but I wore these on our first date. I thought it was appropriate to start our married life wearing them."

Don chuckled, "I remember, Katie."

Don and Kate stopped on the top of the granite steps, oblivious to the world. They sealed their marriage with the first kiss as husband and wife.

The End

Keep reading for a sneak peek of:
Ready to Soar
Book 5
Or **Order Here**

READY TO SOAR: PROLOGUE

*I*t was a glorious day, perfect for a wedding. In a few short hours, Kate's twin brother Shane McKenna would marry Abigail Stevens, Kate's best friend and the love of his life. Kate thought it was amusing that Shane was marrying a girl he'd spent his youth chasing and teasing.

Kate knew the couple was meant to be together. Several months before, Abby and Kate were enjoying lunch when Abby told her that before her mother died she'd told Abby that she would find a place to call home, a place where people cared about their friends and neighbors. And then tragedy struck: Abby lost both her parents and then her sister and brother-in-law, Kelly and Tim, who died in a car accident, leaving Abby alone in the world with the exception of her nephew, Devin. Abby's wedding day would be bittersweet; she missed her family but she was officially becoming a McKenna.

Abby stood in the kitchen doorway wearing a bewildered look. Devin was happily squishing a banana chunk in his chubby hands while the floor was littered with cereal.

Abby wore a sleepy smile. "Please tell me some of that mess made it in his mouth, too."

"Good morning, Abigail. Shane wanted you to sleep in so he gave us a key and asked us to take care of Devin. And we made coffee." Ellie beamed at the little boy. "And we've been having lots of fun, haven't we, Dev?"

Kate poured Abby a mug of steaming hot coffee. "Take a seat. We're starving, so what would you like for breakfast?"

"I'm too nervous to eat. Coffee is fine." Abby giggled. "I didn't expect to see anyone this early. I'll admit it's nice to wake up to calm, smiling faces. Let's enjoy coffee and then, if you don't mind, I'd like to run through the shower. What time do we have to leave?"

Ellie chimed in, "Abby, today is your day and there is no need to rush. I dropped the dresses off at Shane's yesterday."

"Mom, Grace, and Gram have everything under control at the lake. Our job is to get you and Devin to the wedding on time. Don will be over in a bit in case you've forgotten something that has to go out to the lake house today."

The sisters shooed Abby out of the kitchen. "Devin is fine. Go soak in a bubble bath. You have three hours to primp," Kate called as Abby floated on a cloud up the stairs.

"You've thought of everything!" Abby called over the banister. Once again, Shane's family was making the day run smoothly. Her life had changed since moving back to her hometown. It had been a difficult decision to pack up, sell her parents' and sister's houses, and move from the eastern shore to the hills of western Massachusetts. In the beginning, her grief had been overwhelming, losing her parents and sister within a span of twelve months. Abby didn't know how to take care of herself let alone a small child. That's when fate stepped in. Abby and Devin had wandered into What's Perkin', Cari McKenna Davis's coffee shop. Even though it had been years since she had seen her, in typical McKenna fashion Cari welcomed Abby and Devin with open arms.

Abby sank into a hot, fragrant bubble bath, her mind wandering back to those dark days after Devin's grandparents kidnapped him. Edward and Louise Martin had decided Abby wasn't a fit parent. A custody battle ensued, playing out for many long, tense months. In the end, Abby retained custody and was now in the process of legally adopting the boy. The relationship between Abby and the Martins remained strained but tolerable. Today, putting the past firmly behind her, Abby Stevens was starting a future with the man whose heart beat in sync with hers. Shane's family was an added bonus. Instantly, Devin had grandparents, aunts, uncles, and three cousins. Abby's life was turning out just as her mother predicted. Abby pulled the plug on what was left of the bubbles and stepped out of the tepid water to begin the final primping process.

Abby scrutinized her reflection. Short, strawberry blond curls were enhanced with a crystal headband that added a dash of pizazz. Carefully applying her makeup to enhance her blue-gray eyes, Abby used shades of purple and gray eye shadow, dusted her cheeks with f airy pink blush and then a swish of dark brown mascara. Abby Stevens was ready.

Gingerly, Abby took the white garment bag from the closet, picked up the tote bag, and floated down the wide staircase. The moment she stepped into the kitchen a hush fell over the room.

"Abby, you look like a princess," Ellie gushed.

Abby was radiant. "I'm ready."

Don carefully took the garment and tote bag. "I'll put these in the car and come back for Devin's things."

For now, Abby and Devin were moving into Shane's home until they could decide where they would take up permanent residence. Abby loved being lakeside but enjoyed the convenience of town, so everything was up in the air.

"Okay, girls, let's change my last name."

The guitarist was ready and waiting. . .

Abby gave a slight nod. The familiar chords of the wedding march filled the air. Heads turned to catch their first glimpse of the bride. She took a deep breath and nodded to Kate and Ellie. Ellie went first, carrying Devin, followed by Kate and then Abby glided down the flower-strewn path.

Shane thought his heart would burst from his chest. Abby was exquisite. Her long white dress was simple—a scooped neckline, sleeveless—and the sun shimmering off the beading created a vague rainbow effect. Sterling roses completed the picture-perfect bride. If he hadn't already fallen in love with this woman, he would have at that first glance.

Abby's hand was in the crook of Ray's arm. As they entered the gazebo, Abby's eyes locked on Shane, handsome in a dark tux with a lavender rose boutonniere. The sun was dimmed by his brilliant smile. Ray placed Abby's hand in Shane's and took one step back.

The minister smiled at Shane and Abby. "Who gives this woman?"

Ray answered, "I do." He took his seat next to Cari.

The minister moved smoothly through the ceremony while Shane and Abby gazed into each other's eyes. When the minister announced it was time for the first kiss, friends and family cheered and clapped. Devin looked around at the happy faces and he gleefully joined in, clapping his little hands.

Shane and Abby turned to greet their family and guests. Devin strained in Abby's direction so Ellie passed him to her open arms. Shane placed a protective arm around his bride and a steady hand on Devin.

The minister announced, "I'm pleased to introduce, for the first time, Shane, Abby, and Devin, the newest branch on the family tree."

Kate watched her twin, his bride, and their adoptive son. She said a small prayer that they would be blessed to share the same bond in marriage she had with Don, the love of her life.

CHAPTER 1

Kate's dream of a warm sandy beach was interrupted by the shrill sound of the phone ringing. For a split second, Kate wasn't sure if it was real or imagined. Wondering who would call so early, she rolled over and mumbled, "Hello?"

Don pulled the blankets over his head, muttering in protest at the intrusion. He hesitated, realizing she was trying to pass him the phone. "Who is it?" he grumbled.

"It's your mom. I'm having a hard time understanding her."

Don sat up, sleep forgotten. "Mom, what's the matter?" Concern clouded his dark brown eyes. "Is he okay now?"

Kate listened to the one-sided conversation, unsure what was going on but getting the gist that someone had been hospitalized.

"Of course. Kate will need to get coverage at the shop but we'll be there. Either late tonight or first thing tomorrow." He listened to his mother for a few more minutes. "I'll call you when we get on the road, and don't worry, Mom, Dad will be fine, he's strong."

Don disconnected. Kate slid close, wrapping her arms around his waist. The minutes dragged as the couple sat in silence. Kate felt compelled to say something.

"Don, what did your mother say about your dad?"

"Mom called the ambulance last night. Apparently, Dad was having chest pains yesterday while he was working in the vineyard." Exasperated, he continued, "I don't know why he doesn't leave the heavy work to the field hands. But of course, Dad being Dad, he didn't say anything. After dinner, Mom noticed Dad kept rubbing his arm. He claimed he pulled a muscle or something. Mom thought his color was off. That's when she called the ambulance. It was the only way Dad was going to the emergency room. They admitted him for observation and tests but the doctor is fairly certain it was a mild heart attack."

Don looked at his wife. "We have to go see them, and Mom needs me to talk to the doctors. You know my sisters and brothers always expect me to do the tough stuff when it comes to our parents."

"Of course. I'll talk to Mom. I'm sure Ellie and Abby will help." Kate caressed his cheek. "Don't worry, we'll leave right after lunch and be at the winery before dinner." Kissing him tenderly, she flipped back the covers. "I'm going to run through the shower. Why don't you make some coffee?"

Distracted, Don nodded. Needing reassurance, he asked, "Kate, do you really think he's going to be okay?"

Kate sat down on the bed and squeezed his hand. "Donovan Price, other than you, your father is the most stubborn man I have ever met. He'll be fine because the alternative isn't an option for him."

"I know you're right. I can't picture Dad in a hospital

bed. I can't even remember a single time when he was really sick." A deep, ragged breath escaped him. "You're right. Dad will be fine." Don leaned in and kissed his wife. "I love you, Katie."

"I love you too, and try not to worry, we'll get through this together."

Don gave her a little push off the bed. "We'd better get moving. There's a lot to get done in a few short hours. I'll take care of the bed before I make coffee."

Kate dashed into the bathroom, making a mental list of clothes she would need. She wasn't going to have a lot of time to pack before leaving for work, so while hot water ran down the drain she packed her makeup bag.

Kate flipped on the kitchen lights at What's Perkin'. She loved this time of day. Kate tied on a fresh apron and turned on the ovens to preheat, walking through her morning routine helped quiet the worrisome thoughts. What condition would Sam Price be in when they arrived in Crystal Lake? Kate thought about the last time they were at the vineyard. Don and his father had exchanged harsh words regarding his choice to work for Shane's landscaping business. Sam was old school and demanded Don, as the oldest son, return home, and take over the daily operations at the winery. Don loved the growing process—planting and pruning—it was his true passion. Sam said it was time that Don work with his sisters—Tessa would teach him about marketing and Anna, the chemist, would teach him about new wines. His brother, Jackson, was happy to manage the fields; he had no desire to be in charge. Leo, the youngest, had a successful car repair business and preferred beer to wine, so that left Liza, who was happy to stay at home with two small children. Although

Don and Sam left things on good terms, the issue of Don returning to Crescent Lake Winery was unresolved; it was the elephant in the room at every family gathering.

Cari was surprised to find the shop glowing when she arrived. Mouthwatering aromas drifted from the open windows. She discovered Kate up to her elbows in batter. It was clear she had been baking for some time. "Good morning, Sunshine," she called, breezing into the kitchen. Cari got a thrill each morning she entered What's Perkin'. Her hard work resulted in a business to be proud of, and the bonus: she got to share its success with her oldest daughter.

Kate glanced up. "Hi, Mom."

Immediately, Cari could sense something was troubling Kate. "You're here early."

"Sherry called this morning. Sam was admitted to the hospital, and I need to leave after lunch. We're driving to Crescent Lake and we want to get there before dinner. I'm going to call Abby and Ellie. Hopefully they can help with the counter so you can run the kitchen. I don't have any idea how long we'll be gone. It all depends on Sam's prognosis."

Tears filled Kate's eyes. "I'm concerned about Sam, but I'm worried the same old argument about Don taking over is going to come up. I don't want to live in Crystal Lake. Our home is here."

"I thought Don made it clear he wasn't interested."

"Mom, you know my in-laws. The family and winery are everything to them and they've never been happy Don chose to live in Loudon and work for Shane. They put a lot of pressure on him. On us."

Cari nodded. "Honey, I understand about deep family ties, and I have always believed that everything happens as it is supposed to. You and Don need to be there for his family. His parents need your support."

Kate wrapped her arms around her mother. "I know you're right, I'm just scared. What if Sam is really sick and has to retire, or worse?"

"You and Don will cross that bridge when you get to it." Cari squeezed her daughter and smiled. "Why don't you give me the rundown on what you planned for specials over the next few days? It's been a while since I've had the kitchen to myself."

With a slight grin, Kate said, "Just do me one favor, Mom? While I'm gone, don't rearrange the kitchen. It took me six months to get it organized and the flow is perfect."

Amused, Cari said, "You're a little protective of my kitchen, aren't you?"

Kate smirked. "Darn right I am. A chef's kitchen should never be trifled with."

"Not to worry. I promise you'll find everything exactly where you left it. I'm going to call Ellie, Abby, and Grace. I'll have plenty of help."

Cari started the coffee as she thought about her family. There was one thing she was sure about: They always stood together in good times and bad. From the day her first husband, Ben, died, her children cemented their bond. They weren't Stepford children; they fought like cats and dogs but heaven help anyone who tried to hurt one of the McKenna clan. Over the last couple of years, her family had grown. She found love with the man next door, Ray Davis. After they were married, Ray's son, Jake, and his wife, Sara, had triplets, two boys and a girl. Most recently her oldest, Shane, married Abby Stevens and they legally adopted her nephew. The blessings continued to come once Cari had chosen to live in the present and stop grieving for what was lost.

Cari dialed the phone and listened to endless ringing, she was ready to hang up when she heard a breathless, "Hello?"

"Ellie? Is everything okay? You sound out of breath."

"Everything's great. I just got back from a run. Now that I'm finished with school I've decided to exercise."

"Do you want to call me back or, better still, can you swing by the shop before you go to work? There's hot coffee and Kate just pulled cranberry scones out of the oven."

Cari worried about her youngest daughter, a petite blond pixie who looked like a gust of wind could knock her over. But if anyone mistook her for a pushover they would be in for rude awakening. Ellie was a powerhouse in heels.

"Breakfast? Sounds good, I'll be there in less than an hour. I don't have to be at work until late morning and I have an idea I'd like to run past you."

Cari smiled to herself. Ellie was always coming up with new ideas. Since the day she graduated from college, she had been working on, as she called it, her life plan. "I'll be here. Love you, Pixie."

"Love you, too. Bye, Mom."

Next on Cari's phone list was her best friend, Grace. From time to time Grace enjoyed working in the shop, especially when she wanted to get away from her home office and job as a research analyst. Her schedule had enough flexibility to let her come and go as needed. Once Cari explained Kate's emergency Grace said she would stop by so they could set up a work schedule.

Last was Abby. Again, Cari gave a brief summary of

what was going on. "Do you think you could help out a bit?"

"I'm so sorry to hear Sam is in the hospital." Abby empathized with Don. Facing a parent's life-threatening illness was heart wrenching. Her father had a massive heart attack and passed away before her mother, who died from cancer. "What do you need me to do, Mom?"

Cari's heart warmed each time Abby called her mom. Before the wedding Abby approached her future mother-in-law and asked if Cari would mind. Cari said it would be an honor and hoped Devin would consider her and Ray his grandparents. "I was hoping you'd help me bake for the next few mornings, before Shane goes to work. Preparing muffins, breads, and soups would be helpful. Ellie and Grace will cover the front. Ray and the boys will pitch in too if needed."

"I'm sure Sara would like to help if we can get someone to watch the triplets," Abby suggested. "She might enjoy the adult conversation."

Cari hesitated. "You're right, but I'd hate for her to feel obligated. I'll call her later, after I have a schedule. This way I'll know where I have holes. The new office manager Sara hired has her real estate business running smoothly. Good idea, Abby."

Cari pulled out a calendar and penciled Abby in for several early morning shifts. Next, she would figure out when help would be critical for the remainder of the day. The shop should be the last thing on Kate's mind; Don's family needed her full attention.

Kate walked up behind her mother and peeked over her shoulder. The calendar had been divided into sections and initials filled in. Planning was her mother's forte.

"Geez, it didn't take long for you to replace me," Kate mused.

Cari glanced up. "You're irreplaceable, but I've been thinking the shop has grown since the early days. It's apparent we need more than the two of us plus family filling in when we need an extra hand. When you get back we should hire someone for the front and maybe a part-time baker."

"I agree, and we should have talked about this before today. If we had someone trained you wouldn't be scrambling while I'm out of town."

"Don't worry, Kate, emergencies happen. The shop will be fine."

"Hey, Mom. Hey, sissy." Ellie breezed in, dressed in her casual yet elegant country chic outfit. Short blond hair framed her big blue eyes.

Cari knew Ellie took great pains with her appearance and everything she touched.

"Morning, Pixie." Kate smiled at her little sister, who wasn't just five years younger but also the complete opposite of Kate: brunette vs. blond, tall vs. short, and green eyes vs. blue. Despite the differences, the resemblance between the sisters was unmistakable.

"So, what's going on? Why are you and Don rushing off to the winery?"

"Sam was admitted to the hospital with chest pains and they kept him overnight. When Sherry called early this morning, she asked us to come for a family meeting. We don't know if it's about Sam's health or Don and me moving there. Who knows . . . maybe it will be both. But that leaves Mom shorthanded. I'm hoping you'll have some free time to help."

"I'll talk to Karlene. I'm sure I can rearrange my hours at the gallery. Not to worry. I'll make it work."

"Isn't the gallery busy right now?" Cari interjected.

"We opened a new exhibit so the weekends are busy. I have to write another press release for this show to generate some buzz but otherwise there isn't much to do during the week. Besides, we're talking a couple of days, not months."

Kate was relieved. The customers loved Ellie and she could handle the hectic pace, leaving Cari to the kitchen. "Great."

"So, if that's all, can I still have breakfast? Running makes me ravenous and I could eat more than the scone and coffee Mom promised."

"Is that your way of asking for something more substantial?" Kate grinned.

"Well, if you're offering, I'd kill for some eggs, sausage, or whatever is easy." Ellie laughed.

"Come on. I'll feed you before you fade away."

Ellie poured two cups of coffee and grabbed a cookie on her way into the kitchen.

"I saw that young lady," Cari teased. Ellie laughed as she left the room.

Cari was swept up in the morning rush as her attention was diverted to the customers coming and going. Grace stopped by and, as usual, jumped behind the counter to fill orders and ring up sales. When there was a break in the action Cari filled Grace in on the details of Kate's trip. Without hesitation, she agreed to help when the shop was at its busiest.

"Can you start tomorrow?" Cari brushed her bangs back. "This will be just like when we worked in that restaurant that summer during college, remember?"

"What I remember is you made it look easy, you were always chatting up the customers and made great tips. I was a terrible waitress, running around trying to deliver orders, which were usually wrong. Thank heavens I chose the business world. These days I don't have to be nice and/or smile to make money."

"GF, please tell me you'll smile at the customers. If you're lucky you might even rake in some tips." Cari chuckled.

"What time do you need me tomorrow?" Grace hoped Cari would say a time when the sun would already have peaked over the horizon.

"A little before seven? I'll get in by six and get things going. You'll run the counter. Customers start coming shortly after seven."

Grace cringed. "I'll be here. Do I get free coffee?"

"Don't you usually?" Cari smirked as she reached under the counter to hand Grace two dark purple T-shirts.

"I'll see you in the morning, and thanks for the shirts." Grace peeked her head into the kitchen and said good-bye to the girls.

Cari glanced at her schedule. She wasn't worried about the shop but she couldn't shake the feeling Kate might be right. Sherry and Sam had been pushing the kids to move to Crescent Lake and take over the winery since they got married. Don had been working the distribution side of the business when he met Kate. He made the decision to move to Loudon to marry Kate while his brothers and sisters remained happy in their roles with the family business. Cari had no idea what they would decide if the meeting was about Don assuming the position of CEO. It was a difficult situation for everyone.

"Time will tell," Cari mused to herself. She popped her

head in the kitchen. "Ellie, when you're done with breakfast come out here so we can add you to the schedule."

"On my way." Ellie reviewed her mother's notes. "Looks good to me, I'm going to make a couple of copies so I can give one to Karlene but then I need to leave. I hate the hour drive to the gallery, but until I figure out what's next I'm going to soak up all that I can from Karlene—she is a very savvy businesswoman. Not unlike you, Mom. Just a different product." Ellie flashed her dimples as she took the papers into the small office in the back.

"Stop buttering me up, kiddo. Your pay scale is the same," Cari teased.

"Oh, all the food and coffee I can consume? Sweet!" Ellie gave her mom a quick hug and like a whirlwind was off again.

Kate watched her sister leave. "Ellie will never go quietly, will she?"

"No, I don't think so. That's more your speed, Kate."

Mother and daughter grinned and went back to work.

THANK YOU

To keep reading Ready to Soar, book 5 in the Loudon
Series
Order Here

Thank you for reading my novel. I hope you enjoyed the story. If you did, please help other readers find this book:

- This book is lendable. Send it to a friend you think might like it so she can discover me too.
- Help other people find this book by writing a review.
- Sign up for my newsletter at http://www.lucindarace.com/newsletter
- Like my Facebook page, https://facebook.com/lucindaraceauthor
- Join Lucinda's Heart Racer's Reader Group on Facebook
- Twitter @lucindarace
- Instagram @lucindraceauthor

OTHER BOOKS BY LUCINDA RACE:

The Crescent Lake Winery Series 2021

Blends

Breathe

Crush

Blush

Vintage

Bouquet

A Dickens Holiday Romance

Holiday Heart Wishes

Holly Berries and Hockey Pucks

Last Chance Beach

Shamrocks are a Girl's Best Friend March 2022

MORE BOOKS...

It's Just Coffee Series
The Matchmaker and The Marine

The MacLellan Sisters Trilogy
Old and New
Borrowed
Blue

The Loudon Series
The Loudon Series Box Set
Between Here and Heaven
Lost and Found
The Journey Home
The Last First Kiss
Ready to Soar
Love in the Looking Glass
Magic in the Rain

Award-winning and best selling author Lucinda Race is a lifelong fan of romantic fiction. As a young girl, she spent hours reading romance novels and getting lost in the hope they represent. While her friends dreamed of becoming doctors and engineers, her dreams were to become a writer—a romance novelist.

As life twisted and turned, she found herself writing nonfiction but longed to turn to her true passion. After developing the storyline for The Loudon Series, it was time to start living her dream. Her fingers practically fly over computer keys as she weaves stories about strong women and the men who love them.

Lucinda lives with her husband and their two little dogs, a miniature long hair dachshund and a shitzu mix rescue, in the rolling hills of western Massachusetts. When she's not at her day job, she's immersed in her fictional worlds. And if she's not writing romance novels, she's reading everything she can get her hands on. It's too bad her husband doesn't cook, but a very good thing he loves takeout.